FIZZLEBERT STUMP
AND THE BEARDED BOY

FIZZLEBERT STUMP AND THE BEARDED BOY

A. F. Harrold

Illustrated by Sarah Horne

First published in Great Britain in 2013
by Bloomsbury Publishing
This Large Print edition published 2013
by AudioGO Ltd
by arrangement with
Bloomsbury Publishing

ISBN: 978 1471 350849

Text copyright © A. F. Harrold 2013
Illustrations copyright ©
Sarah Horne

British Library Cataloguing in Publication Data available

Printed and bound in Great Britain by
TJ International Limited

For Mrs Coates

CHAPTER ONE

In which introductions are made and in which the reader is welcomed to the book

It began with a pair of false teeth, or rather it began *without* a pair of false teeth.

Actually, now I think about it, that's not exactly the beginning of the story. It might have begun with a red nose. A clown's red nose, the day *that* went missing. But really it began well before that too. I suppose it began with the letter the Ringmaster received one Wednesday morning . . . or maybe it started before that, even.

Oh, beginnings are tricky, aren't they? You think you've got it pinned down and then you look again and there's some loose thread dangling out the other side. You tug on it and soon the whole thing's unravelled on the floor at your feet like a horrible jumper you got for Christmas.

For example, let's say you wanted to tell the story of why you were late for school this morning. You might start by saying you were late because you didn't leave the house early enough. That's pretty straightforward. But why didn't you leave on time? Maybe your little brother was making a nuisance of himself, and you needed to change your shirt because of the porridge. So, that's what made you late. But then, you might ask why the little brat was being so annoying, and it might be because he didn't get enough sleep. There was that thunderstorm in the night and he's so soft that he's still scared of storms. Well, surely *that's* the beginning? But how did the thunderstorm get there? 'There was a cold depression over the Bay of Biscay,' the weatherman might say. 'But, where's the Bay of Biscay?' you might ask. 'Down near Spain,' he might explain.

But even blaming Spain for making you late for school isn't the end of it. Why do you have to go to school in the first place? After all, if you didn't need to go, you couldn't be late. So then you could look back at the history of education and find out who invented the first school (and why they decided it should begin so early in the morning). And on top of that, it might be worth asking your parents some questions. For instance, why on earth did they want to get themselves another child, when they already had lovely little you? And your mother might say that she looked at you as a little baby, fast asleep in your cot, and worried you'd get lonely as you got older, and your father might rustle his newspaper and say that it wasn't his idea.

So, you see, beginnings really are hard things to pin down.

Now I think about it, the missing false teeth actually come later, much later (not until the end of Chapter Seven).

Before that there's a boy I ought to introduce. He's a normal enough lad, about *this* tall and *that* wide . . . But, oh dear, hang on—perhaps I'm still getting ahead of myself. I'm assuming that you know what a boy is. Maybe that's an assumption too far. Let's backtrack a little.

*　　　*　　　*

A boy is like a girl, but not as clean. Like a man, but not as tall. Like a dog, but not as hairy (usually). They wear clothes, run around noisily and wipe their noses up their sleeves.

This particular boy's called Fizzlebert. It's a silly name, I know. But his mum's a clown and his dad's a strongman, so, frankly, he's lucky he didn't end up with an even sillier one. He spends his life travelling with the circus, and since most of his friends are circus acts with all manner of weird and wonky names and titles, he doesn't often think about the *Fizzlebertness* of his name. At least, not as often as I have to.

He's not the one who has to write this book, you see. It's a long word to type, 'Fizzlebert', although thankfully easy to spell, so I shouldn't really grumble. I mean, if I had to write 'bureaucracy' (a word I find almost impossible to spell in one go) on every page, well, then I really would have something to complain about.

But, fortunately, although in all circuses there is *some* bureaucracy, which is to say paperwork, Fizz's story doesn't involve the accountancy department, the Health and Safety inspector's clipboard or the filing cabinet of performers' contracts which sits at the back of the Ringmaster's office-cum-caravan. Or not very much, anyway.

So, where were we? I think we'd got

this far . . .

Fizzlebert Stump (who I most often just call Fizz in order to save on ink) is a boy who lives in the circus. He has a selection of library cards, a pen pal called Kevin, red hair, a dashing old ringmaster's frockcoat, and the ability to hold his breath for just as long as it takes an audience to become impressed by a small boy putting his head in a lion's mouth, and this book is the story of just one of his adventures.

And that's all I've got to say to get the introduction out of the way. Now, roll on Chapter Two, eh?

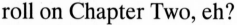

CHAPTER TWO

In which lunch is served and in which some strangers are met

Fizzlebert was sat in the circus's Mess Tent. If you're wondering what a Mess Tent is, then I suppose you've never been in the army, which, looking at you, doesn't entirely surprise me. The Mess is the name soldiers give to the place where they eat, what they call their dining hall or canteen. It's an odd name, especially since they're usually very neat, but the name is the name, sensible or not, and I'm not going to argue with a soldier.

Although a circus isn't an army (it normally has fewer guns and the uniforms are less, well, uniform), the Mess is also what the circus folk call their food hall, or more correctly, their food tent. They do so for much more obvious reasons. (If the reasons don't seem obvious, why don't you give a clown a plate of sausage and mash, a

7

bucket of custard and half a dozen soft boiled eggs, and see what happens?)

Fizz sat at his table stirring a great steaming bowl of stew, dumplings and popcorn. (Cook claimed the popcorn added texture and Fizz couldn't disagree.) Just as he was about to lift the first dumpling to his lips a loud honking made him jump and a pungent waft of mackerel-flavoured air slapped him round the nose.

Fish, the circus's sea lion, was looking up at him with his enormous wet black round eyes. He fluttered his thick eyelashes as if to say, 'Do you have any food to spare, dear sir, for an 'ungry old sea lion?'

Knowing he'd get no peace until the old flipper-flapper had been fed, Fizz offered him the gravy-covered dumpling on the end of his fork.

Fish sniffed deeply at the steaming ball of dough, and with a flick of his head knocked it from Fizz's hand, balanced it, still stuck on the fork, on the tip of his nose, leant back, and flapped his front flippers together with a great wet noise. Then he

jiggled his head from one side to the other, without dropping the fork and dumpling set, honked once and flipped them into the air. They flew high up toward the canvas roof, twirling round and round, before plunging, dumpling first, toward the table.

In a shocking, snapping burst of teeth, Fish caught them in his mouth.

With a twitch of his whiskers and a horrible slurping sound he started chewing. After a moment it became obvious that there was nothing fishy about the stew-soaked ball of flour, and with a loud harrumph and a mordant kipper-flavoured burp, Fish swallowed the dumpling and spat out the fork.

Fizz watched as it flew through the air, spinning and soaring in a graceful arc over the tables and clowns, and landed with a tiny tinny tinkle in the dirt, right in front of a pair of highly polished boots. A little dust and a little gravy splattered across the perfect toes.

Fortunately the Ringmaster didn't notice Fizz's stray fork. He was too busy talking. Talking just loud enough for Fizz to be able to hear the noise, but not to be able to make out the words. It was an annoying way for a man to talk, Fizz reckoned, but then half the grownups he knew fitted into that category: annoying.

Fizz had seen the Ringmaster before. He had seen him almost every day of his life (there was one Thursday three years earlier when the Ringmaster had lost the key to his caravan but even then Fizz had heard him shouting from inside). So he was pretty familiar with how the Ringmaster usually looked and he could tell, from just the merest glance, that today the Ringmaster looked different. His buttons were polished just that little bit brighter, and his boots were polished just that little bit browner and his hair, while not being polished, had been brushed quite thoroughly.

Stood beside the Ringmaster were three people Fizz had never seen before. Having never seen them before, it was impossible for him to say whether they were more highly polished than usual or not, or whether they had brushed their hair in a new and exciting manner, or if, for once in their lives, they'd decided to *not* smear their faces with jam. Those are things you can only say after having known someone for a while and got used to their habits.

That's not to say Fizzlebert couldn't say *anything* about these newcomers. In fact, with just one glance he noticed quite a lot and he could tell, because he wasn't a stupid boy, that there was something not entirely normal about them.

(Fizz always said that he had a special sense for spotting things that were odd, that looked out of the ordinary, un(as you might say)-usual.

11

He called it 'sight'.)

Behind the Ringmaster stood a man of medium height and medium build. (Nothing particularly unusual so far, I'll admit.) He was wearing a shabby brown suit, with wide untidy shoulders. (Lots of people have untidy shoulders.) The hair on the top of his head was thin, but that on his chin was not. (Here we begin to approach the meat and two veg of the matter.) His beard reached right down his chest and was thick and glinted oilily in the shaft of sunlight that hung around in the tent's doorway. (Beards are often a *bit* odd.) It was also blue. Well, it looked blue now, but then, when the man moved his head, the colour changed in the light. The blue was so dark that at times it seemed a shade of black. And then he moved his head, and his beard shifted again, and, for a moment, it looked like it was a rich purple, then black, then blue again.

As beards went, Fizz thought, it was a pretty good one. If rather odd.

But even this wasn't what made him scratch his head and declare the scene one of the three weirdest scenes he'd seen for a week and a half. I've yet to tell you about the *really* interesting bit.

Behind the bearded gentleman stood a lady. She was a head taller than the man, and a fair bit slimmer. She wore a pure white trouser suit, smart and sharp, and was wearing dark glasses. Covering her hair was one of those headscarves like a turban that old-fashioned movie stars used to wear to stop their hair getting all ruffled as they rode in open-top sports cars. And on her chin was a beard, almost identical to that of the bearded gentleman described above. (I'll give you a moment to skip back a couple of paragraphs and reread the bit about the size and colour of his beard. Done it? Fine, let's continue.) Her beard, it should be emphasised, was no shorter, no thinner, and no less impressive than the gentleman's. If anything, Fizz thought, it was probably *more* impressive simply because of whose chin it dangled from.

As he watched she took her dark glasses off (the tent was, after all, much darker inside than the sunny field she'd just come in from) and instead of tucking them away in her handbag or putting them in a glasses case, she slipped them into her silky dark fur of her glorious beard.

Fizz laughed at this, not having seen a bearded lady use her beard as a handbag before (indeed, you could add, not having seen a bearded lady before), but quickly turned it into a cough and covered his mouth with his hand. Laughing at anyone other than a clown (unless they've made a joke or fallen over (without injuring themselves)) is usually rude.

She gave him a hard stare from behind the Ringmaster's back.

(You're probably sitting there thinking to yourself, 'What a magnificent beard that sounds, luxurious and dashing, so beautiful and smooth and elegant,' and of course you'd be right. But as it happens, it's not entirely normal for a beard to find itself on a woman's chin. On the whole, women don't have beards. (I expect they wish they did, but they just can't grow them, at least not until they're really old and have had time to practise.) In previous centuries it was considered so unusual when a woman turned up who did have one that they'd put her in a freak-show and charge people a shilling a time to look at her and point and snigger and gawp. But this is a more understanding age in which you and I live, and we don't have freak-shows any more because we've learnt that no one ought to be pointed at and ridiculed (except clowns), because it's what's inside a person that matters, even if the outside does look a bit . . . different.)

It was only when the bearded lady turned away that Fizz got a good look at the third member of the party.

It took him a few moments to work out exactly what he was looking at.

There was a boy with them, probably about his own age (he guessed from the lad's height), and *his* beard was, perhaps, the biggest and bushiest of them all. It reached down to his knees and spilt out to the sides, even more than the adults' beards did. This was an unruly beard, a beard that had clearly fought against the comb, that had obviously beaten the brush, that was definitely and defiantly doing its own thing. From where Fizz sat it looked a little like an electrocuted badger.

Fizz laughed again, finding this chuckle even harder to hold in.

A boy who meant to be cruel would've pointed and laughed, but Fizz didn't do that. He'd had enough kids take the mickey out of him (once they found out his name) that he kept his pointing finger to himself. It was obvious, all the same, that he was laughing at the bearded boy.

The strange boy glared at him and tugged the woman's sleeve, and she looked over in his direction again.

Fizz shut up. He tried to look serious (which is the worst thing to do when you have a giggle inside you, because it's likely to tickle you while looking for an escape route). He knew he'd been rude, but the boy *did* look silly. Beards are for grown men, he reckoned, and even then they're still slightly silly-looking things. (I disagree with Fizz on

16

this point, as would anyone with any sense of style, dignity and refinement, but we'll let that pass.) No one he could think of in the circus had one (one of the fire-eaters had tried to grow one once, but it hadn't lasted very long). If beards were cool, then surely, he thought, there'd be more of them around?

The Ringmaster, noticing Fizz, brought the strangers over to his table. Fizz wondered if he was in trouble.

'This is young Mister Stump,' the Ringmaster said to the bearded lady (and her men (but she stood in front of them and was quite clearly in charge)). 'He's the son of *The Mighty Stump*.'

'Oh, the strongman?' she said.

She spoke in a voice that sounded smooth and silky like her beard. It slithered into your ears like an expensive wine. Fizz felt it tickled a bit. Which was odd.

'Yes, that's right,' the Ringmaster replied.

'He had a moustache, I think,' she said.

They'd clearly met Fizz's father

18

Mr Stump.'

He had a soft voice that hardly seemed able to climb up out of his throat before it was whisked away on the wind. Soft and quiet and anonymous, quite unlike his wife's.

'Yes, yes,' Lady Barboozul said, turning away from Fizz and looking over at where Cook was ladling food onto people's plates. 'I think we're hungry now. We will take lunch in our caravan, Ringmaster. Have someone bring it over. We can finish the tour later, yes?'

Before the Ringmaster could say anything, she had pulled her sunglasses from out of her beard, slipped them on and began walking back out into the sunshine.

'Gildas, Wystan, come.'

Man and boy lingered for a moment before turning and following her, hurrying to catch her up.

The bearded boy turned back as they went and said, 'I'll see you later, yeah?'

'Yeah, of course,' Fizzlebert answered.

It was only after the boy had said his

21

words and Fizz had answered that he thought about the tone of them. It had sounded a bit like a threat. He'd never had to deal with playground bullies, never having been in a playground, but even without training he could work out the meaning behind the words. It wasn't so much, 'I'll *see* you later,' as it was, 'I'll *get* you later.'

Fizz gulped down half his lunch with a sinking feeling in his stomach. The other half he found he couldn't eat.

*   *   *

Oh dear. Laughing at beards isn't the best way to go about making friends. That's lesson one in this ever so useful book. What could we possibly learn in Chapter Three?

CHAPTER THREE

In which a sea lion chases ducks and in which a clown makes sandwiches

Later on that afternoon Fizz was down by the duck pond (there's always a duck pond in a town park (go look)). He ended up there most afternoons, because Fish liked to swim, but he didn't like to get his spangly waistcoat wet. (Would you want to get duckweed over *your* silver waistcoat?)

Fizz was walking round the pond with the glittering piece of cloth draped over his arm like a waiter in an overly sequined restaurant. Fish was swimming rings round ducks and honking noisily at them from behind. The ducks were spinning round in the water and quacking back at him. (The moorhens had seen the sea lion coming and had rapidly migrated to a park on the other side of town.) It was somewhat cacophonous.

23

And then Fizz saw what he'd been dreading ever since lunch.

His stomach did a little flip and his knees wobbled as if they were thinking about running, but couldn't agree on which direction to head off in. The duck pond noise fell away in his ears.

There, from the direction of the circus, came the shape of the bearded boy. And as it got closer it turned out to be not just the shape of him, but the rest of him too.

'Oi, you!' he shouted as he drew close.

'Me?' asked Fizz.

'Yeah, you. I've been looking for you,' the other boy said, getting right up in front of him.

'Um,' said Fizz, nervously.

'What do you think you're doing?'

'Doing?'

'Yeah, doing!'

The other boy was pushy and angry, and Fizz didn't really know what to say.

'Um, well. I'm holding the sea lion's waistcoat,' he tried, lifting up the spangly bit of cloth.

'What?'

Fizz pointed into the middle of the pond where Fish was balancing a rusty tin can on his nose. 'He likes a swim sometimes, and I . . . er . . . I hold his waistcoat for him.'

'That's stupid,' the other boy said, knocking the waistcoat out of Fizz's hand.

The pair of them looked down at where it had landed on the ground. It lay in a muddle in the middle of a puddle, the sequins spangling glitteringly up from the mucky water.

'Well,' Fizz snapped angrily, 'it's not the only stupid thing round here, is it?'

'What do you mean?'

'Your . . . um . . .' Fizz couldn't say the word, the furry one (you know, anagram of 'bread'). He'd been about to shout it at the boy, but a sudden spark of sense (possibly spelt c-o-w-a-r-d-l-i-n-e-s-s) had flashed in his head. Fizz didn't want to start a fight. In a fight he might get punched, and if he got punched then he might get a black eye, and if he had a black eye his mum would ask where he'd got it and his dad would get all upset and start to cry.

25

And Fizz would have to wear makeup in order to be able to go into the ring to do his act, and he hated wearing makeup (especially when his mum did it for him).

Also, Fizz reckoned being the strongman's son meant that something of his dad's blood flowed in his veins. If the other boy were to punch him, and Fizz accidentally punched him back, he might do some real damage to the boy. (He'd never seen any sign of this super-strength before, but it might be better to try to not get punched, just in case.)

While these thoughts quickly jumped through his head, the bearded boy grabbed hold of the front of Fizz's t-shirt, and tried lifting him up.

This didn't work very well because his t-shirt was a baggy one and needed to go a long way into the air before Fizz went anywhere with it.

'What were you going to say?' the boy said, his blue-black beard bobbing in the bright afternoon sunshine. 'Go on, say it. I dare you.'

Before Fizz could say 'Sorry', which is what he actually wanted to say, the

26

two boys were knocked to the ground by a huge dark wet honking shape.

They both screamed involuntarily and thrashed about underneath the stagnant-smelling sea lion.

Fish barked enthusiastically.

As the two boys scrambled to their feet it was quickly clear the interruption hadn't made the bearded boy any less angry. If possible, it seemed to have had the opposite effect.

'What was that for?' he shouted, pulling a long strand of pondweed from his beard. 'You set your sea lion on me!'

'No, I didn't,' said Fizz. 'And anyway, he's not *my* sea lion. He's his own sea lion. No one tells Fish what to do. I reckon he just saw you and thought he smelt something fishy. He's rather fond of—'

'I don't care what he's fond of,' the other boy shouted, pushing Fizz away. 'He attacked me! I'm going to make a complaint. I'm going to report him and then you'll *both* be for it.'

'Fine,' said Fizz acidly, stepping backwards, his apology forgotten, 'why don't you go running to your weirdy-beardy freaky-furry mummy.'

'She's not my mummy,' snapped the other boy.

'Oh sorry, of course she's not. She looks more like your daddy!'

'She's not my mum,' the lad said, suddenly quieter now, 'and Lord Barboozul isn't my dad.'

'Well, how come the beards match?' said Fizz.

'Yes, well, that's just . . . well, call it luck . . . call it showbiz, if you like. The fact is my real mum and dad are . . . they're dead.'

Gulp.

A pause. Even Fish stopped honking.

Oh dear. Now Fizz felt guilty. He felt bad. He felt small. He'd been taking the mickey out of this boy's beard, teasing him and laughing just because he was different, and now he'd found out that something as dreadful as this had happened to him. Goodness. You should have a go at imagining how you'd feel in Fizz's shoes, because I think, at this moment, he'd be quite happy to swap.

'I didn't know,' Fizz said.

'Why would you?' said the other boy, kicking at the ground and looking at his feet.

'What's your name?' Fizz asked, trying to keep his voice from wobbling.

'Wystan,' said the other boy.

'Wystan's an odd name,' said Fizz. 'I've never met a Wystan before.'

'You're Fizzlebert, yeah?'

'Yes. It's an even odder name. You can laugh if you like.'

'Nah,' Wystan said. 'There's nothing wrong with odd, is there?'

'No, of course not,' said Fizz, feeling

29

terrible. 'Tell me about your . . . your mum and dad. I mean, if you want to.'

'There's not a lot to be said. There was this . . . this accident and . . . well, their hot air balloon just never came down. The police looked for months but they never found it. I was left an orphan and they, I mean, Lord and Lady Barboozul, they took me in. They were friends of my parents. Old friends, they said. They'd even been there when I was a little baby.'

Suddenly Fizz laughed without meaning to. He clamped his hand over his mouth.

'What is it? What now?' Wystan snapped, almost angry again.

'Oh, sorry!' Fizz said, totally shocked with himself. He was blushing deep red. 'I didn't mean to . . .'

'No, go on. What made you laugh?' Wystan prodded Fizz in the chest with his finger.

Fizz nervously began to explain. He twiddled the hair at the side of his head as he spoke, and half wished he had a beard of his own to hide behind.

'I just thought,' he said slowly,

tiptoeing through the words as if walking through a minefield in a cow pasture (any step might go 'splat' or 'boom'), 'that if your real parents had asked Lady Barboozul to look after you, I mean, asked her back when you were a baby, then . . . then, she might actually be your godmother.'

'Yeah, I think she is,' Wystan said, staring suspiciously over his beard. 'What of it?'

'Well, in that case, you could say,' Fizz said slowly, 'that she's your . . . furry godmother.'

There was yet another silence. Fish looked from one boy to the other, whiskers glistening in the bright afternoon sunshine.

Then Wystan smiled. (Fizz noticed it around his eyes before he saw it round his mouth, which is often the way when a bearded person smiles.)

And then he laughed.

And then both boys were laughing.

'That's an awful joke,' Wystan gasped. 'Are all your jokes that bad?'

'Most of them,' Fizz said. 'Mum's the funny one really.' He felt so relieved that he went on, 'Hey, why don't you come back to my caravan before the show?'

He held out his hand.

And Wystan, after a moment's thought, took Fizz's hand, shook it and said, 'Yeah, okay.'

*   *   *

Fizzlebert lived with his parents in a small caravan. His bed folded down over the dining table, and the kitchen sink doubled as the bathroom sink when he had to brush his teeth. It wasn't big, but it was home to him and that was what mattered.

His mum, whose clown name was *The Fumbling Gloriosus*, was called Gloria, but I'm going to call her Mrs Stump, because it's more polite.

It was an hour before curtain up on the evening's show and she was wearing her brightly coloured clown costume, but hadn't yet done her makeup. When Fizz and Wystan appeared, she offered them some sandwiches and poured two glasses of lemonade, with straws and everything.

'Thanks Mrs Stump,' Wystan said politely, 'but I can't eat the sandwiches.'

'Why not?' she asked. 'Don't you like ham and jam?'

(Even without her clown face on, she had some funny ideas about what made a proper sandwich. Rhyming fillings were an especial favourite: she did a great peas and cheese roll, of course, and also a (slightly soggy but ever so yellow) mustard and custard baguette.)

'It's not that I don't like ham and jam,' Wystan said, looking a little sheepish. 'It's just that I'm not s'posed to eat when there's people around.'

'Why ever not?' Mrs Stump asked.

'Food gets stuck,' he said.

'Stuck where?' Fizz asked.

'In here,' Wystan answered, patting his beard. 'Lady Barboozul says it's disgusting, and that no one ought to see a beard full of sauce and breadcrumbs and bits of carrot. I always eat by myself. That way I can brush out the crumbs before I meet anyone.'

'Well, we've got napkins, you can always wipe it up as you go,' Fizz's mum said.

'No. It's embarrassing. I'm sorry, Mrs Stump, it does look a nice sandwich.'

The two boys noisily sucked their lemonade.

'Do you drink soup through a straw as well?' Fizz asked.

'I've not tried it, but it's an idea,' Wystan said.

While the two boys chatted at the dining table Mrs Stump wrapped the sandwich in some paper so Wystan could eat it later, and began painting on her clown face at the other end of the caravan.

'Wystan?' came a voice from outside.

The face of Lady Barboozul appeared in the doorway.

'Have you got Wystan here? Ah, there you are, boy. Lord Barboozul was worried.'

'I was playing with Fizz,' he said. 'His mum made sandwiches.'

'Sandwiches?' She sounded slightly shocked.

'I didn't eat them. Don't panic.'

'Good. Quite right. But you shouldn't be bothering Mrs Stump like this. Come home now.'

At the sound of her name Mrs Stump stood up. She banged her head on a shelf, knocked a cuckoo clock with her elbow so it began cuckooing, and accidentally tapped the tap on the sink as she reached over to shake Lady Barboozul's hand. Water squirted into the basin, where there were some bowls waiting to be washed up, and the curve of the topmost bowl sent the water spout fountaining out of the open window.

There was a shocked shout of surprise from outside as someone got it in the eye.

'Hi there. I'm Gloria, Fizzlebert's mum,' said Fizzlebert's mum, Gloria, holding her hand out for the bearded woman to shake.

Lady Barboozul looked at it as if it were the hand of a fishmonger who was allergic to gloves. And washing.

'Yes,' she said cautiously. 'I'm afraid I don't shake hands with clowns. I had a . . . an experience once.'

Mrs Stump shrugged her shoulders, honked her horn miserably and slouched away to her dressing table to finish applying her eyebrows. She looked devastated.

Fizz wasn't upset for her, though. He knew that she was just playing the part of the dejected clown, because that was what happened when she was in makeup: things always went wrong for her (she was called 'Fumbling' after all) and she'd slouch off sulkily until something went even more wrong (or 'wronger' if you prefer) for one of the other clowns, at which point she'd slap her sides and point and laugh. Usually she laughed heartily until a bucket of whitewash landed on her head or a custard pie hit her, when she'd become all sad and put upon again. Clowns are just like that. You shouldn't take them too seriously.

Wystan whispered mischievously, 'The clown had a joy buzzer in his hand. They give you a sort of electric shock when you touch it? Lady Barboozul's beard went crazy . . .'

'Wystan,' she said quickly. 'No one wants to hear about that.'

Mrs Stump had perked up at the story and her bow tie was twirling.

Wystan went quiet. 'Sorry,' he muttered.

'Quite right, boy,' Lady Barboozul said. 'Come along. We must prepare for our first show. Must make it look good tonight, yes?'

Then she surprised Fizz by squeezing past the two boys sat at the little dining table and leaning over to his mum. Her beard only just avoided trailing in Fizz's plate with its breadcrumbs and jam smears. If Fizz hadn't known better he'd've said that it had lifted itself up to avoid the plate, but beards don't do that, so it must have been an illusion.

'It was good of you to look after Wystan,' she said to Mrs Stump in a sweet warm voice. 'I'm glad he's made a friend. So rare, isn't it? Thank you.'

And before Fizz's mum could answer, she retreated, turned and strode out of the caravan, pulling Wystan along behind her.

And then the two bearded marvels were gone.

Mrs Stump said goodbye with a mournful sliding note on a miniature swannee whistle, and turned back to her mirror.

Fizz saw that Wystan had left his sandwiches behind, and while his mum was busy, ate them himself.

*   *   *

I'll grant you, it's perhaps not the most cliffhangery ending to a chapter, a boy eating a sandwich while a nearby clown finishes her makeup, but I think if I was trying to eat I'd like a bit of peace and quiet before the next chapter begins. So please, be kind, and give a Fizz a moment to ingest (which just means 'eat' with more letters, like what a postman does) before reading on.

CHAPTER FOUR

In which a strongman is surprised and a nose goes missing

Fizzlebert was just wiping the last crumbs from the front of his t-shirt (looks like you waited long enough before starting the chapter—we both thank you) when his dad appeared in the caravan doorway.

'Hi Fizz, had a good day? Where's your mum?' he asked, enthusiastically.

'Hi Dad,' Fizz answered with a sigh. 'I don't know where she's got to.'

(He pointed to the cupboard above the sink.)

'That's strange,' his dad said, grinning widely. 'She's normally here.'

'Yes,' said Fizz, talking like a bad actor. 'I don't know where she could've got to.'

'It's not like her to go missing.'

'No, Dad.'

'I'm worried about her, Fizz. Where

40

could she be?'

'I'm sure you don't need to worry, Dad. She'll turn up. Why don't you have a cup of tea?'

(He carried on pointing at the cupboard above the sink.)

'A cup of tea?'

'Yeah. You'll need to get the tea bags though.'

'Oh, okay,' said Mr Stump.

Fizz clicked the switch on the kettle and his dad put a pair of mugs on the table and opened the cupboard above the sink, where the teabag tin was kept.

As the long horizontal door was opened a brightly-coloured silk-clad shape rolled out and fell into his arms. It was Mrs Stump, laughing loudly and honking her horn.

'Boo!' she shouted between giggles and wriggles.

Mr Stump put her down on the floor.

'Oh Gloria!' he said, laughing his deep barrel-bellied laugh. 'You really got me that time! My heart fair jumped out of my chest. Such a surprise! I had no idea you were hiding up there.'

Mrs Stump slapped him with a

kipper.

'I love you, Herbert,' she said. (Herbert was Mr Stump's middle name.)

'I love you too, Gloria,' Mr Stump replied.

'I'm going to be sick,' added Fizz, sticking his fingers in his ears.

*   *   *

This happened every single day. Being a clown, his mum loved surprising her husband, and so whenever she got the chance she hid. However, she'd been doing this for years and since (a) anything that happens every day for

42

years soon ceases to be a surprise, (b) hiding places in a caravan are limited, and (c) no one wanted to hurt anyone else's feelings, Fizz and his dad had had to grow very good at *pretending* to be surprised.

The kettle boiled and Mr Stump made two cups of tea, while Fizz poured himself another lemonade.

'Have you heard the news?' his dad said as he stirred his tea.

'What news?' asked Mrs Stump, now back at her dressing table where she was adding the finishing the touches to her clown face.

'The Circus Inspectors are coming on Saturday.'

She put down the grease paint stick and turned to look at her husband. 'Really?'

'What's that mean?' asked Fizz. 'Who are these inspectors?'

'They're from the British Board of Circuses. They're officials. They have clipboards.'

'Yes, and red pens, too,' added his mum.

'They decide whether a circus is any

good or not.'

'What? How? Why?' asked Fizz, not sure which question he wanted to get out first and so blurting a little bit of each of them all at once.

'Well,' said his dad, 'they just watch the show and see if it's any good. Sometimes they look around backstage too, to make sure it's all safe and what-have-you. Sometimes they ask questions. Every Inspector has his or her own way of testing, that's what they say. It's usually pretty easy. Nothing to worry about.'

His mum gently honked her horn in agreement.

'We've never failed one yet, have we dear?'

She honked again.

'No. I've been in circuses for twenty years or more,' his dad said, 'and I've never once been reprimanded, down-graded or expelled. Not once.'

'Expelled? What does that mean?' said Fizz beginning to feel worried.

'Well, that only happens in the most extreme cases,' Mr Stump said. 'When things are seriously bad and the acts are rotten. Sometimes, the Circus Inspectors will recommend an act be removed from the circus and sent back to Civvy Street. Sometimes, if it's really bad, the whole circus might be expelled. Closed down, you might say. Demobbed.'

'Civvy Street? Where's that?' Fizz asked.

'It's nowhere, Fizz,' his mum said.

Fizz didn't like the sound of being Nowhere. It sounded dull.

'It's not a real place, son,' his dad clarified. 'Civvy Street just means the world outside the circus. Expelled acts get dumped out there and are given ordinary jobs. You know, they're made to be accountants or shop assistants or the people who tidy up the leftovers in restaurants. Boring jobs. Normal jobs. "Just stuff" sort of jobs.'

'You mean,' Fizz said, gulping, 'not circus jobs?'

'Exactly. That's it.'

'And these Circus Inspectors can do this to a whole circus?'

'Well . . .' his dad began in a thoughtful tone.

'*Monty Marsh's Mirabelles,*' said his mum.

'What?'

'She's right,' Mr Stump said. 'They stopped touring about six years back. Never heard from again. Never mentioned again in the British Board of Circuses Weekly Newsletter either. Just vanished.'

'And that was 'cos of these Inspectors?' Fizz asked. He thought he'd heard of all the circuses that were out on the road (*Auntie's Amazing Antipodean Acrobatics* and *Frobisher's Freak-O-Rama-Land* and *Simon's Simple Circus* and *La Spectacular De La Spectacular De La Rodriguez' Silent Circus Of Dreams* and so on), but he'd never heard of *Monty Marsh's Mirabelles*.

'Well, the Circus Inspector's bad report is just one theory,' his dad said. 'Some people say Monty retired to open an outward bound centre in North Wales, and some people reckon he never could read a map right and is still out there somewhere looking for the next town.'

46

'But what do you think, Dad?'

'I'm with your mum, Fizz. A Bad Report.'

Fizz was in a lather now. He thought about the act he did with Charles, Captain Fox-Dingle's elderly lion. Would it be enough to impress these Inspectors?

'Easy-peasy,' his mum said, adding an upward toot on her swannee whistle.

'What?' Fizz said, startled out of his thoughts.

'There's nothing to worry about, Fizz,' his dad said. 'Your mum's right. This circus will pass easily. We've got some great acts going on. I've been lifting heavier things than ever, and your mum's at her very clumsiest. And then there's the new act.'

'You've heard about them?'

'Yes, I met them this afternoon. I don't know what they do, but the Ringmaster said it would knock my socks off.'

'But you don't wear socks,' Fizz said.

'I told him that, and he said he'd lend me some.'

Fizz cracked a small smile at that,

47

but couldn't help the panic that was swimming through his head making it onto his face round the edges (and over a fair bit of the middle too).

'Fizz,' his dad said, 'we're going to be fine. I remember the last time the Circus Inspectors came. Three boring blokes with clipboards at the back of the Big Top. It was ticks all the way. We'll pass with flying colours, just you wait and see.'

Although Fizz trusted his dad, he determined at that moment to do his part in making the circus the best it could be, and to make sure that his act was as good as ever, if not better. He had a horrible picture in his mind of the family being kicked out of the circus. They'd end up living in a brick house that never moved, with the same view out the window every day, and he'd have to go off to a boring grey school while his mum and dad carried grey briefcases off to their offices and made him eat cabbage and fish fingers for tea. No candyfloss, no sea lions, no acrobatics, no fun.

But if his mum and dad weren't

worried, he wouldn't worry. Not yet. Not for now. There was no need, was there?

'I hear it's sold out tonight,' Mr Stump said, changing the subject. He meant the Big Top would be absolutely full. 'Should be a good show, eh? You and Charles been practising, Fizz?'

'Yes, dad, we're ready. The Captain is trying out a new toothpaste, so I should be able to keep my head in there for even longer,' he said. 'Catch the custard tonight, Mum!' (There are superstitions in show business. Actors, for example, never say 'Good luck' or 'Have a good show', instead they say, 'Break a leg'. Clowns say even funnier things, including what Fizz just said.)

There was a silence where there would normally be a horn honk.

'Gloria,' said Fizz's dad, 'Fizz said, "Catch the custard tonight"?'

She didn't answer, again.

Mrs Stump was busy rummaging through the drawers of her dressing table, throwing the contents left and right over her shoulders. Fizz could tell this wasn't simply the usual untidiness

49

of a clown.

'Mum,' he asked anxiously, 'what's wrong?'

She honked once as she paused in her search and pointed at the middle of her face.

Oh!

Her nose.

Her face was all painted, and she'd pulled her frizzy yellow wig on, but the red nose that should have sat at the middle of it all was nowhere to be seen.

Fizz's mum didn't need to say

anything for Fizz to know what this meant. But since you've probably never lived with a clown, I will.

A clown's nose is as much a symbol as it is a real thing. It's their badge of office, you might say. A clown treasures his or her nose. It is precious to them. It is what they are awarded at Clown College (instead of a certificate) when they pass their exams. To have a nose (and not just one of those cheap plastic ones anyone can buy in a joke shop, but a real handcrafted specially-fitted-by-an-expert one) is what every hopeful student clown is aiming for.

Someone just wandering into Fizz's caravan and seeing that Mrs Stump had lost her nose might suggest to her that she borrow a nose. They might point out that Larry Yellow, *The King of Custard*, had got concussion when he dropped an invisible ball on his head yesterday and was laid up in bed. His nose is going spare tonight, they might say. Why not ask him if you could borrow it?

If they did suggest that (oh dear, oh dear, oh dear), they would be met with bemused, puzzled, dumbfounded stares from both Fizz and his parents. What a silly suggestion. What a bizarre, weird, downright stupid idea.

A clown's nose is as individual as their face. No two clowns have the same one. They're like fingerprints. They're unique to the clown whose nose the nose nuzzles. They're like underpants. You simply don't lend them out. You don't ask for a borrow. It's an absurd idea.

And besides, it probably wouldn't fit.

By now Fizz's mum was frantic. (She tried pulling her hair out, but settled for just taking her wig off.) Both Fizz and his dad were looking too, through drawers and on top of shelves and in the sink and under the table and behind one another. None of them could find it.

Outside a hush fell and then the band struck up the opening fanfare. In the Big Top the evening's show was beginning.

Mr Stump had to go because this evening he was the second act on, but Fizz stayed for a while to help his mum look. She knocked things over and he rummaged through the piles.

After a fruitless twenty minutes Mrs Stump sat down at her dressing table in the middle of all the chaos and began wiping off her makeup. Without her nose she couldn't go out in public. Without her nose, she wasn't even a *real* clown. Other clowns wouldn't recognise her. They wouldn't include her in their act. That was the Clown Code: '*No one knows one with no nose on.*'

Fizz tried to cheer her up by looking on the bright side. 'Maybe it'll be nice to have an evening off?'

And she looked at him with her real face which looked even sadder than her sad clown face had looked, and she sighed. She didn't believe Fizz. (Fizz didn't really believe Fizz either.) She loved being a clown. Tonight no one would laugh at her, no one would clap her, no one would remember her.

'We'll find it tomorrow,' Fizz said, hopefully, 'and then you'll be back in the ring. Better than ever.'

She honked her horn quietly and

tried to give him a bit of a smile.

*   *   *

Not a hundred yards from the caravan the show has begun. Later on Fizz is going to do his trick with Charles, the lion, but before that everyone who's spare is gathered either backstage or out in the aisles of the audience waiting to see the first performance of the *Great Barboozul Family Frenzy of Fur, Fear and Fun*, the new act.

And I have a sneaking suspicion that's where I'll be for the next chapter. It'll be more fun than hanging around with a noseless clown.

CHAPTER FIVE

In which some beards are exhibited and in which a boy is shot from a cannon

Fizz got ringside just in time to catch the end of Dr Surprise's daring display of magic and mind-reading. (He correctly guessed the name of a small girl randomly picked from the audience (even though she had only volunteered when her mum loudly said, 'Go on Debbie, put your hand up, he might pick you'), and then he pulled a rabbit from his hat, some celery from behind her ear and a modest round of applause from the crowd.)

The Ringmaster walked out in his smart red coat, with his polished boots and his top hat with the red ribbon, and made the announcement Fizz had been waiting for.

'Ladies and gentlemen, boys and girls, budgies and giraffes, Brian and Geraldine. It is our great honour to give you a brand new act never before performed under the canvas of this, or any, Big Top. An act so full of daring, mystery and downright fear that I must issue a warning beforehand. If there is anyone here of a nervous disposition, who is afraid of the unusual, or who is anxious around the bizarre, then this is the time to close your eyes, put your fingers in your ears and hold tight to your mummy's hand. For anyone still looking, I give you *The Great Barboozul Family Frenzy of Fur, Fear and Fun!'*

The crowd clapped and cheered and fell silent as the lights in the Big Top dimmed into darkness.

The band struck up a mysterious winding tune, all exotic and odd sounding. A pair of spotlights began roving round the sawdust of the ring.

One caught on the corner of something and stopped.

There was a creak from the stalls as the audience leaned forward in their seats to see what it was.

There, in the middle of the small circle of light was a foot. Wrapped around the foot was a dark boot and as the light began to creep upwards it became obvious the boot was on the end of a leg and then that the leg was beside a second leg and that they were both covered by a long coat.

The light edged upwards and just above the bottom of the coat was the frondy end of the blue-black beard Fizz had been expecting to see.

It seemed to twist and ruffle in the white light, as if it were alive.

The light inched further up the beard, up and up and up.

Fizz should've seen the face of one of the Barboozuls by now, but this beard seemed to go on forever.

The beard was three feet long, then four feet, then five feet, and still the spotlight went up.

The endless coat shimmered behind the glossy purple-black, blue-black furriness of the beard as if it were sewn with sequins or crushed jewels, and the beard itself seemed to be shimmering as it shifted about like a bed of black worms or a river of dark furry snakes.

Eventually the spotlight stopped on a head. It must have been twelve feet in the air. Fizz thought he recognised Wystan's face underneath the top hat that topped the figure off, but wasn't sure, not until the band burst into a blaring upbeat, jolly, vigorous circussy tune.

As it did so Wystan leapt from the top of the elongated person, like a squirrel off a trampoline, landing in the sawdust with a forward roll, his beard springing out into its usual unruly shape.

Behind him the tall figure tottered and wobbled, its super-long beard still in place.

Fizz recognised the thinning hair on the newly exposed head and guessed that Lord Barboozul was sat on top of Lady Barboozul's shoulders. Somehow his beard hung low enough that it mingled with hers, making it look like one giant beard hanging from his chin. Clever stuff.

One of the spotlights followed Wystan as he did acrobatic rolls and handstands round the ring, and after a particularly impressive backflip he surprised everyone by landing in the audience. He grabbed the hand of a young girl who was sat in the front row and pulled her after him back into the ring.

The crowd applauded as they always do when someone volunteers (especially when their volunteering is less than voluntary).

Fizz had been watching his new friend being brilliant and was surprised by a loud bang as a cracker went off with a great blast next to the strange double-height Barboozul. A great gush of smoke whooshed up and hid them from view.

Lady Barboozul stepped out of the cloud looking elegant and beautiful in a glittering white dress. Her beard was jet black against the bright frock, and she held a smooth pale hand out to the young girl.

She giggled nervously before taking hold of it. Lady Barboozul turned her round to face the crowd, who applauded again.

She was wearing jeans and a t-shirt, with a pair of scuffed trainers and a green jacket. She had a neat blonde fringe and was looking both scared and excited, as well as uncertain as to what to do.

She didn't see Lord Barboozul appear out of the quickly clearing cloud of smoke behind her.

He was dressed like a magician: a smart dinner jacket and incredibly well-ironed trousers. There was, presumably, a bow tie, but no one but a barber would be able to find it under his beard. As he walked forward he held his hands in the air, showing them off to the audience, in the way a magician shows you the nothing-up-his-sleeves before he produces a pound coin from behind your ear.

He held his hands still. They didn't move.

But his beard moved.

Everyone could see that.

As the crowd watched, puzzled and shocked, his beard dipped into the girl's jacket pocket, like a searching pair of fingers or inquisitive furry tentacles, and when it came out it was holding a camera by the strap.

He'd just pick-pocketed her with his

beard!

The crowd was silent, but in a good way.

Lady Barboozul whispered something to the girl and everyone laughed as she put her hand in her jacket pocket and found her camera gone. She looked worried, puzzled, amused.

Lord Barboozul knocked the camera against his head as if to prove it were real. And then, with Wystan pointing at it so that no one could miss what was happening, he put it *inside* his beard.

He held his hand up to show it was empty.

Lady Barboozul slid her hand deep into *her* beard and pulled out . . . a bunch of flowers. They were the usual paper flowers that magicians produce from up their sleeve and it was clear that the audience weren't very impressed.

She handed the flowers to the girl and reached into her beard again. Her arm vanished right up to the elbow and when it came out it was holding a violin. The crowd 'oohed' at that. Hiding a violin in a beard is pretty impressive.

She gave the girl the violin to hold and had a third rummage.

This time Wystan helped her. What they pulled out was the end of a ladder. Wystan took it and walked away from her as she fed out rung after rung, until he was holding a ladder all of four feet long. I'll admit, four feet isn't very long for a ladder, but for a ladder hidden in a beard, it's rather good.

As Wystan took the ladder off into the dark toward the back of the ring, Lady Barboozul pulled one final thing out of her beard.

The girl, who had tucked the violin and flowers under her arm, jumped and clapped her hands together.

Lady Barboozul gave her her camera back.

Once the audience had settled down Lady Barboozul took hold of the girl's arm and guided her fingers into her beard.

She pushed further and further into the fur, just as the bearded lady was urging her to, and soon her whole arm was in there.

But it didn't come out the other side.

Instead, it came out of Lord Barboozul's beard, even though he was standing six feet away.

The amazed crowd clapped and roared their approval, especially when the girl waved and watched her own fingers all the way over there waving back at her.

As the crowd died down she pulled her arm out, the hand vanishing from Lord Barboozul's beard and reappearing on her wrist where it belonged, and he led her back to her mum, who was sat with her mouth open in the audience.

Fizz was sat with his mouth open too. He'd seen women cut in half before (and, happily, put back together), and Dr Surprise could make his rabbit disappear inside his hat, but never had he seen someone's arm travel between two beards. That had to be as impressive as sticking your head in a lion's mouth, surely? Maybe even more. He was feeling a little worried now. Would the audience expect him to pull things out of Charles's mouth later on? Would they be disappointed when he couldn't?

The music rose as the lights came up at the back of the ring.

Wystan was stood there with the ladder. Silence fell as the audience saw what it led to.

A cannon, Fizz thought. Oh no!

(Fizz had once heard his mum and dad talking about a human cannonball who had been with the circus years ago. He no longer worked there because he'd been fired.)

Wystan climbed the steps and strapped a helmet onto his head.

A stage hand lit a long fuse at the rear of the cannon. It fizzed and sparked.

Wystan climbed into the cannon's mouth and lowered himself in feet first.

Back in the ring Lord and Lady Barboozul faced one another. His beard reached out and took a hold of hers and as they backed apart the two tangled beards formed a woolly night-black ribbon of rippling fur between them.

The audience didn't know where to look. And now even Fizz wasn't sure where to focus his attention. All he knew was that this was one of the best things he'd seen in the circus in his whole life. It was exciting, confusing, dazzling. He and Charles couldn't compete with this. And he thought of his dad lifting giant weights and juggling concrete blocks, and realised there was no comparison there either. And clowns? What did clowns have on these magic beards?

He was jealous and happy and amazed and upset, all in one confusing emotion. What would Wystan think of him when he saw how boring Fizz's act was?

A deep cracking boom made him look up as Wystan went flying out of the end of the cannon in a cloud of white smoke with arms whirling and legs dangling behind him.

The boy landed in the middle of the Barboozuls' combined beards, which stretched like an elastic band and poinged the boy back in the opposite direction.

Once again he flew through the air, arms doing their cartwheels, and whooshed straight out the large curtains at the back of the ring. That was where the acts waited their turns to go on. Fizz wondered if anyone had got hit.

From his seat at the edge of the ring he saw the curtain swish open and the short form of the undamaged boy, his newest friend, the wonderfully brave Wystan, come running out, holding his helmet up in one hand and waving to the audience with the other.

Lord and Lady Barboozul met him in the middle of the ring and the

three of them took their bows to a tremendous round of applause. The clapping seemed to go on and on. Fizz had hardly ever heard it so loud. There were even people standing up and clapping.

To a certain extent Fizz agreed with them, the act had been . . . wow! The circus was lucky to have found these Barboozuls, he thought, especially with the Inspectors coming the day after tomorrow, very lucky indeed. It certainly meant the rest of the acts would be trying their hardest to look good alongside them, but he did have a worry at the back of his mind. If the circus had acts this good, then might the day come when they didn't need him to stick his head in a lion's mouth?

*   *   *

Later on that night Fizz was just hanging around behind the Big Top with Fish watching Miss Tremble (who was in charge of the circus's horses) singing to the horses (it calmed them down after the show and some of them refused to go to sleep if she didn't do it) when a couple of kids and their parents saw them and wandered over.

'Oh, you're the boy who put his head in the lion's mouth, aren't you?' said one of the boys.

'Yes,' Fizz said, always happy to be noticed. 'That was me.'

(Occasionally you get fans coming backstage and asking for your autograph when you work in a circus. It's just one of the things that happens. It's no big deal. The public are naturally awestruck and want a little bit of you take home with them, so they can remember you later on.)

'We was wondering if . . .' the other boy said.

His mother nudged him and said, 'Go on, ask him . . . he won't mind.'

Fizz noticed the lads had their autograph books and he reached into the inside pocket of the ringmaster's coat he wore and fumbled around for a pen.

'Yeah,' the boy said again. 'Um . . . do you know where the boy with the beard is?'

'Oh,' Fizz said, pulling his empty hand out of his coat. 'No, I think he's gone to bed.' (This wasn't exactly a lie. The Barboozuls had certainly gone to their caravan, and although Wystan Barboozul might not actually be in bed, the rule in a circus is that once a caravan's door is shut for the night, you don't disturb it (except in case of fire, flood or for a celebratory hot chocolate when someone's unexpectedly given birth).)

The kids sighed, scuffed the dirt and turned back to their parents, who said, 'Thank you anyway,' over the kids' heads and wandered off.

Fizz was left with the awful sound of Miss Tremble singing and the awful feeling of unsigned autographs. And then Fish burped and the atmosphere got even worse.

It was a rather miserable end to a day and to a chapter, especially after the excitement of the Barboozuls' act. I promise to not get so gloomy again, not for a few chapters anyway. The next one's quite jolly, really.

CHAPTER SIX

In which some football is played and in which a scream is heard

The next morning Fizzlebert was sitting at the dining table (which was also the kitchen table (and the coffee table)) dipping his candyfloss into his bowl of cornflakes and nibbling them off. (His dad said this saved on the washing up. He didn't like washing spoons. Very few people do.)

Fizz had slept well and was telling his mum about the Barboozuls' act for the third time, and how much the audience had loved it. (He left out the fact that he felt his act hadn't gone so well.) His mum was usually all ears for circus gossip (she had a pair of huge plastic ones she put on if the gossip got especially juicy) and the idea that she might not want to hear how well the show had gone without her didn't occur to him. At least, not until his dad

71

nudged him in the ribs and gave him a special look which said, '*Son, remember your mum's lost her nose and wasn't able to perform last night. Perhaps she doesn't want to know how well everything went without her, hmm?*' It was quite a special look, but Fizz had seen it before and understood it immediately. He felt an idiot for having forgotten.

He tried to be more sensitive.

'It was good,' he said. 'But it wasn't a *funny* act, Mum. I mean no one was laughing at it. It really could've done with a bit more slapstick.'

'Really, honey?' his mum said, playing with her coffee cup.

'Yeah, of course,' Fizz said. 'I mean, what's an amazing magic beard compared to a custard pie?'

'Humph,' she said, slumping in her seat.

There was a knock on the door.

It was Wystan.

'Hi, is Fizzlebert there?' he asked, in a bright furry voice.

Mr Stump said he was, and Wystan asked if they could go out and play together.

Fizz had never had a friend of his own age in the circus before. Nobody had ever come calling for him. He rather liked the feeling.

He asked his mum if it was alright to go out.

'Yes love,' she said. 'Of course you can. Just remember you've got a lesson with Dr Surprise at ten o'clock.'

That was over an hour away.

(It's probably worth remembering that even children being brought up in circuses have to have lessons, and Fizz had his with the various members of the circus who knew about certain subjects. Dr Surprise was supposed to be teaching him History, although more often than not they ended up discussing magic tricks and books.)

Wystan had a football and he and Fizz took it into the bit of park between the circus and the duck pond for a kick-about.

'You were brilliant last night,' said Wystan.

'What do you mean?' asked Fizz, wondering if his bearded friend was taking the mickey.

'Sticking your head in the lion's gob. Talk about brave! It's madness!'

'Oh,' said Fizz, feeling slightly confused. He hardly considered it brave. He'd been doing the act with Charles for ages and it seemed perfectly normal to him. The lion had a set of rubber false teeth, he explained, so even if he did bite down on Fizz's head, all he'd be able to do was suck him a bit. It wasn't nice, but it didn't hurt very much. Nobody's ever been gummed to death by a lion.

In a circus a lot of things are illusions like that, are tricks. As long as they look real to the crowd, they've done their job.

'We're thinking of putting magic into the trick,' Fizz added. 'Dr Surprise is going to teach me to pull Flags-of-all-Nations out of Charles's mouth while I've got my head in there. That should liven it up a bit, don't you think?'

'I like it the way it is,' Wystan said. 'It's a good trick. I wouldn't mess it about too much.'

'Thanks,' Fizz said, modestly brushing the compliment aside, 'but I reckon what *you* did with the cannon, now that's *brave*.'

'Ah, but that's a trick too,' Wystan said. 'Watch from backstage tonight and you'll see how it's done.'

'Cool,' Fizz said. He liked knowing how tricks were done, and was always badgering people to show him new ones. He could do a number of card tricks and produce a bunch of flowers from his sleeve if you gave enough warning (an hour or two).

It was odd, Fizz thought, but now he knew Wystan thought what he did was impressive, he had already begun to feel a bit better about himself.

'Your dad,' Wystan asked casually as they kicked the ball back and forth. 'How strong do you reckon he is?'

'How strong? Well, I've seen him lift a motorbike once . . .'

'That's pretty strong.'

'. . . with the rider still on it, and he was one of those big guys, you know, with a fat belly and tattoos and a big beard.'

'A big beard, really?' Wystan said.

'Yes. Oh!' Fizz had almost forgotten

75

his friend's beard. Like sticking your head in a lion's mouth, it's strange how the strange can become normal simply by your being around it a lot. 'I didn't mean anything . . .'

'Don't worry, it's okay.'

The two boys carried on kicking the ball about until Fish got in the way, stole it and started balancing it on his nose.

'He loves balancing things, doesn't he?' Wystan said.

'Yeah,' Fizz agreed. 'It's about all he *can* do. That and find fish.'

At the sound of the word 'fish' Fish let the ball drop to the ground and waddled over to Fizz, expectantly.

'No, no fish, Fish,' Fizz said, shaking his head and holding up his empty hands.

Fish snorted a salmon-flavoured snuffle and slowly, his head hung low with seafood-starved sadness, began the long waddle back to the circus.

Wystan watched wide-eyed.

'The poor thing,' he said.

'Oh, ignore him,' Fizz said. 'He's just putting it on. He's the best actor in the circus.'

'I saw most of the show last night,' Wystan said, running to collect the football which was rolling towards the water's edge, 'but I didn't catch Fish's act.'

'Act?' Fizz asked.

'Yeah. Is it good?'

'Fish?'

'Yes.'

'Oh, Fish doesn't have an act.'

'But he's got a spangly waistcoat. And he had a top hat on yesterday, didn't he?'

'I think he just likes dressing up,' Fizz said. 'He doesn't actually *do* anything. He's a sea lion.'

'But why's he in the circus if he doesn't have an act?' asked Wystan.

The truth is, no one knew where Fish had come from. He'd just turned up one day. He could balance things and honk enthusiastically, so he seemed to fit in with the circus crowd, but the one time the Ringmaster had tried to get him into the ring to do something, Fish had got halfway out and had frozen. It was a terrible case of stage fright,

people said.

(Unnecessary Sid, a clown, had nudged Bongo Bongoton when he saw this and said, 'Fancy putting some chips on, to go with the frozen Fish?')

He had sat there, staring up at the lights and at the crowds and refused to budge, and a sea lion who doesn't want to move isn't going to be moved by the likes of you or me. They're heavy things, and stubborn.

Fizz's dad had had to come out and pick him up and carry him out of the ring. He got a nasty nip on the ear for his troubles. (If you look closely you can see the scar.)

Since then no one had suggested Fish try to become a star again.

But they still threw him fish and he still balanced anything he could get his nose under. They liked him. After all, there *was* that time he'd chased away the burglars who'd tried breaking into the Ringmaster's safe, and there *was* the time he'd rescued Fizz from Mr and Mrs Stinkthrottle, and there *was* that time he'd rescued the whole salmon from Cook's worktop. But those are different stories.

As Fizz explained all this, somewhere across the park a church bell rang ten times. Fizz was late for his class and ran off toward Dr Surprise's caravan, leaving Wystan to carry the ball back to his parents' caravan. They promised to meet up again later on.

*   *   *

'Oh woe! Oh tragedy!' moaned Dr Surprise, when Fizz knocked on his caravan door.

'What's wrong?' he asked, as he

climbed up the steps.

Dr Surprise was sat on the edge of his bed with his face in his hands, moaning loudly. The *Famous Performing Rabbits of the World* duvet cover was all rumpled up and there were playing cards and plastic flowers spilt on the floor. The stuffed crocodile that hung from the ceiling was dusty, as if it hadn't been cleaned for days. In short, the place was less tidy than normal.

'Oh dear, oh dear! Oh, woe is me! No, no, no!'

The Doctor was almost entirely bald, except for a few long strands that usually wound their way round the top of his head and flopped down pointily above his left eye, but this morning they were flapping uncombed in the air. His tight black suit, which squeaked ever so slightly when he moved, was covered in dust and straw, and his tie was undone. His moustache drooped down in a depressed dangle. (It was a plastic moustache. He had a collection of them, and wore whichever one best matched his mood.)

'Oh, Fizzlebert,' he said, looking up with a jump. 'I didn't hear you come in.'

'Dr Surprise,' Fizz asked anxiously, 'what's the matter?'

The Doctor wiped his eyes and took a deep breath.

'It's Flopples,' he said. 'She's not well. Not well at all.'

Flopples was his rabbit, the one he did the magic tricks with. She usually lived inside his top hat. If you watched carefully, sometimes, when he was sitting down for dinner in the Mess Tent, you'd catch him poking a carrot up inside. If there weren't many people around he'd take his top hat off and put it on the table and she'd look out with her little paws on the rim and watch what was going on. Fizz had often slipped her a bit of lettuce (which she seemed to like, even when Chef had dipped them in a toffee sauce). It was a way of clearing the salad off his plate without having to eat it himself.

Dr Surprise lifted his hat up from the floor, where it had been sitting between his pink fluffy bunny rabbit slippers.

Flopples was curled up asleep at the bottom of it, and even Fizz, who was no expert on rabbits, could tell she wasn't feeling well.

For a start, she was green.

'Take a look at this,' the Doctor said, passing Fizz a plastic box.

It seemed to be full of gravy. Fizz sloshed the brown soupy liquid around a bit. It had a few strands of grass in it and smelt unpleasant. He asked what it was.

'Droppings,' Dr Surprise said.

'Droppings?' Fizz asked. 'You mean Flopples' droppings?'

Anyone who knows anything about rabbits is well aware that a rabbit's . . . 'leavings' are small and dry and round. They're firm, usually neatly piled, and easily confused with chocolate chips when baking.

One thing rabbit droppings shouldn't do is slosh, and another thing they should never do is splash.

A rabbit with diarrhoea is not good news. It's a much messier animal, for a start, and not, Fizz thought, the sort of pet a man would want to keep in his

82

caravan, let alone in his hat. And, for another thing, it's almost impossible to spell. You'd think as the author of this book I'd be able to tell you that Flopples had a much simpler illness, say, a cold. A cold only has four letters, and almost everyone knows which ones they are, but diarrhoea has loads and they look like they've been dropped on the floor. I'd rather he had a rabbit with bureaucracy, even, but the fact of the matter is, as your author, I can only tell you the truth, and the truth is that Flopples had the illness I mentioned before. The one that has too many vowels. Begins with D. I wrote it down before. I won't do it again.

'See? She's not well at all,' the Doctor said, interrupting my lengthy complaint. 'My poor Flopples. My poor baby. Her stomach's all round and about, and she's not touched her breakfast.'

'What's wrong with her?' Fizz asked. 'Is it something she ate?'

'I don't know. I've phoned for the vet, but he can't get here until this afternoon. Until then all I can do is

keep her warm. Keep her safe.'

He started sobbing again, removed his moustache, blew his nose on a hanky Fizz gave him, and then replaced his moustache.

'But you,' he began between sniffs, 'you didn't come here to see a grown man cry. You've come for your history lesson, haven't you?'

Fizz nodded slowly.

He didn't much care for lessons. They were always about things that were less interesting than almost anything else in the circus or that he read in a book for himself. Who needed to know, for example, about wars that had been over for hundreds of years, when you could be learning about how to shoot a boy from a cannon and catch him in your beard without hurting anyone?

'Dr Surprise,' Fizz asked, trying to put off the history moment for as long as he could, 'how long has Flopples been sick?'

'When I got up this morning she was like that. Green. And mucky. I washed her and cleaned out the hat. And she . . . she's just been sleeping ever since. The poor mite.'

'What happened? I saw her during the show and she was fine then, wasn't she?'

'Oh yes, perky as a button. She got all the answers right. The crowd loved her, Fizzlebert. She was an absolute star.'

'And then what happened?'

'Um. After that we watched that amazing new act . . . do you remember? The one with the beards in? Weren't they good? And after *that*, we came back to the caravan for our cocoa.

We're working on a new trick and wanted to practise it a few times before bed.'

He paused and scratched at his head, as if he were trying to remember.

'You see,' he went on, 'I thought if I mixed a Larkin's Luminous Larker with a Furious Finnegan's Fanfare (that's the one with the sparks and the noises like trumpets), then I might be able to get a sparking smoking glowing musical hat.'

'That sounds brilliant. Did it work?'

'Well, I got it glowing and I got it sparking, but the trumpets are proving harder to control. They refuse to stay in tune.'

'Is that what's made Flopples ill? A glowing hat?'

'Of course not. I've been using my spare top hat for that.'

Dr Surprise pointed at a slightly fizzing battered old hat that sat on the draining board.

'Well, did anything else happen?'

'We were trying the trick and then that woman came to say how much she'd liked the routine we'd done, and . . .'

'Woman?'

'You know Fizzlebert, the new woman. The one with the . . .' He pointed at his chin.

'Lady Barboozul?'

'Is that her name? I don't remember. Terrible head for names, me. Well, she told me how much she liked our act. She was ever so nice and very polite. Kind. She reminded me a little of Dr Surprise, except . . . for the beard.' He tilted his head thoughtfully and his monocle glinted like a winking eye. (His wife, who Fizz had never met, had been a doctor too, just in case you thought he was being reminded of himself, which he wasn't.) 'She sat down and I let her hold Flopples for a bit as we chatted about this and that. All very civilised. After she'd gone I gave Flopples her supper and put her water bowl down and went to bed myself.' Dr Surprise paused and looked into his top hat, where the poor rabbit was still snoring quietly. He sighed and spoke again. 'And then . . .' he said.

'Yes?'

'. . . and then I got up and she . . . Flopples . . . she was . . . she was coughing and coughing, Fizz, and . . . and she sicked up this horrible claggy fur-ball, and just sat there panting and wheezing . . . and now . . . well, now she's just sleeping . . .'

'Oh, Dr Surprise! Don't worry,' Fizz said. 'I'm sure she'll be better soon.'

'But Fizzlebert, you don't understand. We've never missed a show before. If she's not feeling better by tonight, we can't go on. I can't work without her, she's my everything.'

Fizz patted the Doctor on the shoulder and said that everyone needed an evening off now and then. Besides, come the morning, of course Flopples would be back to her old self.

But he wasn't nearly as sure as he sounded.

Dr Surprise wasn't in the mood for a history lesson that morning, and (not unusually) neither was Fizz, so he made his apologies and left the Doctor to wait for the vet.

Fizz was sat on the steps outside Dr Surprise's caravan, thinking about the poorly rabbit and his mum's missing nose, when a sudden cry split the sunny morning and echoed round the circus. It was a horrible wail of pain and was accompanied by a quieter crunching sound and then by a crash and then by a whimper.

He looked all around, trying to work out where it had come from. And then he ran off in search of the source, leaving us hanging around here at the end of the chapter waiting for someone to turn the page and read on.

CHAPTER SEVEN

In which a Strongman is
weakened and in which
a trick is revealed

Fizz arrived at the scene of the scream just in time to find his dad being lowered onto a stretcher by a pair of first-aid giving clowns.

'Ooh,' said Mr Stump painfully as they laid him down on the canvas and put a blanket over his chest.

The clowns took up positions at either end of the stricken strongman, bent down and lifted the poles that supported the stretcher.

There was a ripping sound and they walked off in the direction of Mr Stump's caravan with the poles, but without the stretcher and Mr Stump, who were still on the ground.

When they were safely out of the way, Mr Stump said, 'Fizz, help me up will you?'

Fizz took his dad's hand and helped

him hobble to his feet.

The strongman pressed one of his great big hands to the small of his back and tried stretching.

'Aarggh.'

'Have you done your back in, dad?' asked Fizz. 'Was that what the scream was?'

'Scream?'

'Yeah, I heard a scream.'

By now a small crowd had gathered round the two Stumps.

Two more clowns came forward with a big bag of first aid gear. One of them pulled a stethoscope out and tried to listen to the side of Fizz's head. Fizz brushed him away. The other one was already tangled up in the bandages he'd begun unrolling and ten seconds later was lying on the floor looking like a muddy mummy with a quietly honking horn and a red nose poking out between the wrappings.

'I don't scream,' Mr Stump said firmly. 'That was Madame Plume de Matant. I was lifting her up.'

Madame Plume de Matant was the circus's fortune teller. She had a little

tent of her own that visitors could visit
before they went into the Big Top. She
would tell them their futures, which
mainly involved saying, 'You are going
to see a circus,' in a French accent.
(People sometimes complained that
that wasn't what they'd paid a pound to
hear, but however much they argued,
they couldn't fault her predictions.)

'You dropped her?'

'I don't drop things,' Mr Stump said,
sounding like he was either cross or in
pain or both.

'Why did she scream then?'

'Because she fell,' Mr Stump said quietly.

'Because you dropped her, dad?'

'Sort of. Ooh.'

The strongman was tottering back to his caravan leaning on Fizz's shoulder. He was a big man and Fizz was only a short lad, so they were moving quite slowly. His back was obviously badly twisted.

'Why did you drop her?' Fizz asked. 'I mean, "sort of" drop her.'

Mr Stump stopped walking and his son stopped with him.

He looked down into the boy's eyes and said, 'You mustn't tell anyone, Fizz. They'll laugh at me.'

'Okay. I promise.'

'I lifted her up, and was just getting ready to start juggling, when I was . . . tickled.'

'Tickled? You told me you weren't ticklish. You said grownups aren't ticklish, that it's something kids grow out of!'

'Well, sometimes adults can be tickled, but only if they're surprised. Not normally.' He turned and gave Fizz a look as if to say that this was information not to be abused, but as he turned there was a popping sound and the look he gave included more pain than was intended. 'I was tickled,' he went on after a moment, 'and I wriggled and my back went pop and then Madame Plume de Matant fell on top of me and we both fell down. She wasn't hurt, but I couldn't move at all. Ooh!'

'Who tickled you?' Fizz asked.

'Well, that's the thing, son. I never saw. While I was lying on the floor, I

94

looked around, but there was no one there. But I swear I was tickled by something.'

'Maybe it was a feather blown by the wind.'

'Maybe,' his father agreed.

However much sense it made, it was clear this solution pleased neither of them.

*   *   *

The two Stumps got back to their caravan and Mrs Stump had her husband lie down on the hard floor and stretch, just in case it helped.

'That's your father out of action,' she said to Fizz. 'Last time his back went it took a month before he was able to lift a broom, let alone a car.'

'But what about the Inspectors?' he asked hurriedly. 'Flopples is sick too and your nose ...'

'I know, Fizz. We turned the caravan upside down this morning looking for my nose. It's not here. I've had to order a new one. The woman from the Clown-U-Factory is coming tomorrow to measure me up. But it's still going to take a week to make. This family isn't having the best of luck, Fizz. Your mum and dad aren't exactly doing much for the circus, are we? It's lucky we've still got you and Charles in the ring.'

'But, will you get expelled? I mean, if you can't perform?'

'Oh no,' Fizz's dad said from the floor where he was lying. 'I don't think it works like that. They'll judge the circus as a whole, probably. I doubt they'll ask about us. I mean they can't judge an act they can't see, can they?'

'I suppose not,' Fizz said, unsure whether that really made sense. 'But . . .'

'Well,' Mrs Stump said, 'if you're worried, you'd best make sure you and Charles put on a blinder of a show tonight. Yes?'

'Oh yeah, of course,' he said. 'I'll make you proud.'

He wished he'd meant what he'd said, but after all that had happened, the good effects of Wystan's pep talk had evaporated. Fizz began to worry, not just about his act, but about the others too. If things carried on like this, Fizz thought, the circus might run out of acts altogether. And then the Circus Inspectors, with their clipboards and their red pens, couldn't give a Good Mark, could they? Where would the circus be if that happened? On the scrapheap, or working in a supermarket putting price stickers on tins of beans, or doing photocopying in a local council planning department office. It didn't bear thinking about, thought Fizz, as he thought about it.

*   *   *

Fizz watched that evening's show from the darkness behind the curtains backstage. He could see the acts just as well as you could from any seat in the audience, except everything was backwards. That is to say, he saw backs more than he saw fronts and bottoms more than he saw tops. But still, it was enough for him to know what was going on.

He was still excited about the

97

Barboozuls' act, even while worrying about the rest of the stuff. He really wanted to know how they did all that beard stuff, not to mention Wystan's trick with the cannon. This evening it was definitely a different girl that he plucked from the audience, and Lord Barboozul stole a notebook out of her pocket, not a camera, but Lady Barboozul still produced it from her beard.

Eventually Wystan climbed up the ladder onto the platform near the rear of the ring. Fizz watched as he slid himself into the cannon's barrel. He listened to the fizzing fuse and counted down the seconds before the explosion.

As it went off, a little door opened at the back of the platform and Wystan slid out. With the boom and the gush of smoke all the attention of everyone in the Big Top was focused on the flying figure which burst out the cannon's mouth, and Wystan nipped through the darkness and in behind the curtains to where Fizz was stood.

'You'd best duck,' he whispered to his friend.

Fizz felt Wystan's beard tickling his ear as he spoke.

The two boys ducked down just in time.

Wh-i-i-i-i-zzz!

The bearded boy who'd just been shot from the cannon hurtled through the narrow gap in the curtains, straight over their heads.

He crash-landed a few yards away, all mangled and higgledy-piggledy. Fizz's stomach leapt into his mouth as he watched the figure sliding along in the dirt and spinning round. He'd seen lots of people fall off things in his time, but acrobats always knew how to land safely and they didn't do it like that.

But then he thought a second, even more obvious thought, which was that Wystan, the bearded boy, the lad who had climbed into the cannon, was actually stood next to him, hand on his shoulder, with a big smile on his face.

'See,' Wystan said, laughing. 'I told you there was a trick to it.'

Fizz looked at him and looked at the boy on the ground and then looked back at him.

'Huh?' he said.

'You'll see. I've got to go now. Fizz,' he added before he went back through the curtains into the circus ring, 'sorry to hear about the lion.'

Suddenly Fizz was on his own.

Wystan was back in the ring, taking his helmet off and waving to the crowd.

Fizzlebert wandered over to where the other Wystan was lying in the dirt.

It was a dummy.

Well, of course it was. Fizz kicked himself that he hadn't thought of it earlier, that he hadn't spotted it the night before. Letting a dummy take the flight in Wystan's place was much more sensible. But Fizz still couldn't imagine how they did the other tricks.

And then something waved at him from inside his brain. It was something someone had said that he hadn't paid attention to at the time. What was it?

Um.

Something about . . .

No. It was gone. But it sniggled in Fizz's head, just out of reach, going, 'Look at me, listen to me, remember me!'

You know how sometimes you want to say something and can't quite get the right word out? It's a word you know, and probably one you've said hundreds of times before, but it just sits there like a bubble of forgetfulness in your mouth, and you say, 'Oh, it's on the tip of my tongue.' Well, that was exactly what Fizz was feeling, except it wasn't on the tip of his tongue, because he didn't want to say it out loud, just remember it, so instead he was thinking, 'Oh, it's on the tip of my brain,' which is similar to the tip of your tongue, just about four inches further back.

He was interrupted by Captain Fox-Dingle.

'Fizzlebert. No teeth,' said the Captain, who always kept things brief.

It was hard to hear him over the applause that was coming from the other side of the curtain.

'Sorry?' Fizz asked him. 'What did you just say?'

'No teeth, Fizz. No teeth, no show. Charles. Gummy. Teeth?' He pointed at his mouth. 'Missing.'

Fizz added up the words and made them into something like a sentence. His heart sank. Charles's rubber teeth were missing, and if the lion didn't have his set of rubber dentures, then they couldn't do the act.

For a split second Fizz thought they could use Charles's other false teeth. But then he remembered how Charles tore open great hunks of meat with them and thought better of it.

Fizz was gutted. (Though not as gutted as he might've been, had he attempted the trick with a suddenly sharp-toothed lion.) He'd just listened to his friend get the biggest round of applause he'd heard for ages for not-actually-being-shot from a cannon, and now he couldn't get *any* sort of round of applause, because some false teeth had gone missing. It wasn't fair.

He was angry. He felt robbed.

He kicked at the ground.

'Sorry. Me too,' said a glum Captain Fox-Dingle, touching the buttons that gleamed on his chest.

He meant he was hurting as much as Fizz was, that he felt useless missing the show too.

Fizz wondered how he'd break the news to his mum and dad. The Stump family were now entirely pointless as circus performers. If the Inspectors saw them all sitting around doing nothing, Fizz was sure they'd be demoted or expelled. How could they not be? He felt bad thinking how bad they'd feel when he told them and that made him feel even worse.

And then he remembered what it was that he'd forgotten.

'Sorry to hear about the lion.'

Wystan had said that to him.

It was a simple enough comment, of course. The sort of thing a friend would say to another friend. But how had his friend known about the missing teeth before Fizz did?

The Barboozuls had come off stage now, and were being congratulated by various people on another fine show. The Ringmaster had a big grin on his face. He ruffled Wystan's hair and slapped Lord Barboozul on the back, and went to slap Lady Barboozul on the back too, but stopped when she looked at him from over the top of her beard.

Fizz gave Wystan a puzzled look, and Wystan waved back, smiling.

And then Lord and Lady Barboozul whisked away back to their caravan and took their bearded boy with them.

Fizz was left standing on his own in the middle of all the busy backstage bustle, putting things together in his mind. He promised himself to keep an eye on those beards. He had the feeling that something weird was going on. All this bad luck, and at this important time? It couldn't be natural. A seed of suspicion had sprouted inside his head and was tickling him behind the eyes and between the ears.

*   *   *

Do you remember on the very first page I said it began with false teeth, or rather *without* false teeth? Well, it turns out I was right. Now the story has really begun. Finally. Or rather it will begin in the next chapter.

CHAPTER EIGHT

In which a panicked look is spotted (or maybe it isn't) and in which plans are hatched

The next morning the Ringmaster called a meeting. Everyone gathered together in the Big Top. Well, everyone who could.

Mr Stump's back was no better, so he stayed on the floor in the caravan. Dr Surprise refused to leave Flopples on her own. (Fizz had popped in to take him some breakfast. The rabbit was less green today, but still off her food.) And several clowns were stuck together outside their caravans and couldn't come either. (They'd been practising custard throwing and one of them had thrown a bucket of glue someone had left lying around.) The circus's stilt-walkers stood at the front of the crowd, their stilts having vanished in the night.

'My friends,' the Ringmaster began, 'this is a big day for us. Saturday.

We've two shows to get through, the matinee this afternoon and then the big show tonight. Tomorrow we pack up and move on, so let's make today special. As you know, we're also expecting the Inspectors today. They could be watching either show, or both. Since we've got a few new faces in the circus since the last inspection I'd best tell you what to look out for. Circus Inspectors look like normal people, on the whole, only they almost always carry clipboards. They love their clipboards. I heard of one Inspector who used to take his in the bath with him, but he also inspected aquariums, so maybe that . . .' The Ringmaster trailed off absentmindedly, before beginning again. 'Ahem, so just make sure you're nice to everyone you meet today, just in case they've got a clipboard hidden away somewhere.'

He looked as his notes and added, 'Of course, a few accidents have happened, so I'm having to do a bit of juggling.' (There was a little ripple of applause when he said that. It had been years since the Ringmaster had juggled in the show. In fact it was back before he became Ringmaster, when he'd been just plain *Jimmy Woosh the Juggling Bush*. People were excited to think they might get to see the Ringmaster stick some twigs in his hat and get juggling again. But it wasn't to be.) 'No, no, no,' he went on, hushing the applause. 'I mean *rearranging*. I'm going to have to move some acts around. I've written it down here, so come and see me afterwards to get the details, but I'll just say, after two spectacular shows, I've decided to move the Barboozuls to the end of the second act. They're an ideal strong finale.'

At this news everyone turned to give a round of applause to the bearded threesome who were stood at the back. Lord and Lady Barboozul hadn't been listening. They'd been whispering to each other and the sudden noise made them jump.

They smiled (their beards rose at the edges, where the corners of the mouth go up) and Lady Barboozul waved delicately at all her fans. Thank you,

she seemed to be saying.

But Fizz, who had been watching them ever since they'd all come in thought he saw something else.

He reckoned she'd looked panicked when everyone had turned round. Panic is something that shows in the eyes. If you have good self-control you can stop your hands shaking, you can control your frowning, you can seem utterly calm even if you're babbling inside, but the thing that twitches first when panic hits is the eyes and no one can control that, not immediately. It takes a second or two to get them under control, to blink away the shock, and Fizz was sure he'd seen her twitch. Not even a beard could hide those eyes.

Could it be that under that smooth voice, that calm and polite voice, she was actually wicked and controlling and set on destroying the circus?

Fizz shook his head. The bearded family were the circus's best hope (perhaps even their only hope) for impressing the Inspectors. They were sure to get the circus a Good Mark. How could they be behind the accidents? Was it just to make themselves look even better in front of the Inspectors? That didn't seem likely to Fizz for two reasons: firstly, they had an act that stood out even among the circus's other great acts, and secondly, and more importantly still, a circus was a team, it was a family. In a circus people cared for one another, not about making themselves brilliant, but about making the whole show brilliant. A circus was full of nice people, and everyone seemed to think the Barboozuls fitted in.

His mum had said nice things about

110

them when they sent his dad a 'get well soon' card the evening before. The Ringmaster obviously thought they were real circus folk, or he wouldn't have hired them in the first place, or moved them to the headline slot.

Even Dr Surprise had said how nice Lady Barboozul had been when she'd come to visit him. Why, she'd sat down and stroked poor Flopples. That wasn't the sort of thing a villain does, Fizz reflected. I mean, what villain's ever sat down and stroked a pet?

But as he thought that another thought popped up alongside and waved at him.

Had *she* poisoned Flopples?

Had she *poisoned* Flopples?!

Fizz gasped as he thought the thought. It shocked him, just the thought of thinking it. She wouldn't! She couldn't! But Dr Surprise *had* said Flopples had coughed up a fur-ball. And who is better placed to give a rabbit a fur-ball than a friendly bearded lady?

The Ringmaster had started talking again, and Fizz was the only one still

111

watching the Barboozuls.

He saw Lady Barboozul whisper something to her husband and she nodded in the direction of Percy Late, of *Percy Late and his Spinning Plate* fame. Her husband nodded and smiled and then slipped out the back of the tent.

Wystan was stood in front of his guardians and seemed to be falling asleep as the Ringmaster droned on. Did Wystan know? Was he protecting her? Was he just pretending to be his friend? He'd asked all those questions about Fizz's dad, shortly before his dad was tickled. Was Wystan in on it all?

The Ringmaster finished his speech by saying, 'Ladies and gentlemen, you all know what we've got to do today. Eat well, practise well, and perform well. This is the one that really counts. This is our future. So remember, let's be careful out there.'

As they all shuffled out of the tent Fizz's head fizzed like a sherbet hand grenade. He couldn't just tell someone. He knew what grownups were like. They wouldn't believe him. He needed to find evidence, and if he couldn't find proof, then he needed to at least find a pair of rubber false teeth so that he and Charles could do their act tonight.

Since it was Saturday he didn't have any classes, which meant he had four hours before the afternoon show began. That had to be long enough to do something, surely. But what?

If you had a thermometer and were able to hold it close to Fizz's head, you might note a small increase in temperature as his brain began thinking extra hard.

*   *   *

Half an hour later he was feeling both better and worse about things. He was walking between caravans looking for Percy Late (with or without his Spinning Plate) and while he walked his brain was still steaming, trying to piece together the jigsaw of clues he'd found. He'd visited the glued-down clowns and had been to see Dr Surprise again, where after a disgusting investigation he was more certain than ever that something was definitely going on. It wasn't just bad luck.

'Fizz! Hey, over here!'

Wystan was calling him.

Fizz pretended he didn't hear.

He really didn't want to talk to Wystan. He didn't want to find out that his newest friend was involved. And if he wasn't involved, then that was almost even worse, he didn't want to have to tell Wystan that his parents were causing all the chaos.

In a way Fizz was angry at Wystan for being an awkward lump in his path. He didn't mean to be angry, didn't want to be angry, but he couldn't help it. The secret knowledge he had was tearing him in two and the easiest way to not be tugged apart was to simply walk away and try to forget about Wystan for the time being.

'Fizz!' called the bearded boy, puffing slightly as he came running over. 'Wait up!'

Fizz only stopped walking when he felt the hand grab his shoulder.

'What do you want?' he snapped at the bearded boy.

'Um. I just wondered if you wanted to . . . you know.' Wystan held up the football he'd been carrying under his arm. 'We've got a couple of hours, haven't we, before lunch?'

'Oh, have we?' Fizz said sarcastically.

Wystan pulled his sleeve up so they could both see his watch. 'Yeah, look,' he said.

'Well, no. I don't think so,' said Fizz.

'Oh, okay,' said Wystan, a little sadly. 'Are you busy?'

'Yes, as a matter of fact I am,' Fizz said angrily. 'I'm trying to work out why you want to ruin my circus.'

He hadn't meant to say it. Well, not quite like that. Part of the plan he'd almost come up with was to search for clues and evidence quietly and subtly, before accusing Lady Barboozul in front of the Ringmaster and whatever remained of their fellow circus performers.

'What do you mean "ruin the circus"?' Wystan asked.

'Ever since you got here,' Fizz said, standing with his hand on his hip, 'everything's gone wrong. You come round for tea and then Mum's nose goes missing. Dr Surprise's rabbit coughs up a fur-ball, right after your mum's been to visit him.'

'She's *not* my mum.'

'Well, whatever she is, she's bad news. I've looked at the clowns. The ones who glued themselves to the ground this morning. And do you know what I found stuck in the glue? A long black hair.'

'So what?'

'It was long and bluey-black. It was hers, wasn't it? Or maybe . . . maybe it was yours? Why are you all trying to ruin our circus?'

Fizz blurted this out almost without thinking. It was true though, what he'd said about the clowns. He'd found that one long black hair stuck in the glue. And Dr Surprise and Fizz had looked through his rubbish bin and found Flopples' fur-ball. (This was not the most pleasant of jobs.) Pulling on an end each, they had unwound it and found that it was just as long and just as black as the other one.

Now he was on his way to see Percy

Late, who lived on the other side of Captain Fox-Dingle's cages. The Barboozuls had been looking at him in the meeting and Fizz had a feeling he was to be their next victim.

But Wystan looked so shocked, so surprised, so upset, by Fizz's accusation, that Fizz's heart began to melt a bit.

'I thought we were friends, Fizz?' Wystan dropped the football and stepped right up close, so his beard fluffed in Fizz's face. 'Friends don't accuse each other of things. Friends don't make up stories like that. Why would we want to break your circus? I mean, look at it. It's a rubbish circus. It's the worst circus we've ever worked. It's a pushover. Your clowns aren't funny. Your lion's got false teeth. Your plate spinner only spins one plate. And your flipping sea lion doesn't even work. If we did want to break your circus, we wouldn't have to try very hard, would we?'

With that Wystan pushed Fizz out of his way and ran off into the maze of caravans, leaving Fizz stood on his own. His ears were bubbling and his legs wobbled underneath him. He gritted his fists and wished he had something to throw. Not something heavy, just a bit of mud or a snowball or something. Just something he could chuck in the direction Wystan had run to show that he was angry. Grrr!

He felt like shouting, 'If our circus is so rubbish, how come we won a Silver Rosette for *"Generous Amounts of Excitement"* at the British Board of Circuses All-Circus Circus Show last year?' (which was true, if a bit long for a snappy retort) but he didn't. Maybe if there'd been anyone there to

118

hear he might have, but they would've needed to have heard the rest of the conversation in order for his comment to make sense, and grownups are rubbish at listening. They never seem to hear the words, just the noises the words make. All they would have noticed was two boys having a row, and they would've patted them both on the heads, ruffled their hair and said something stupid like, 'Oh come on lads, shake hands and make up, eh? It can't be all that bad, eh?' That was the sort of things adults said. Idiots.

Fizz suddenly remembered that he had to find Percy Late before his practice session began. He ran off through the caravans towards where the great plate spinner was parked.

*　　　*　　　*

Being on time had never been Percy Late's big talent (plate spinning wasn't Percy Late's big talent either, but let's not be mean). Fizz was hoping he'd be late today (Late, that is, not Fizz), but Late wasn't late, he was on time for once, which meant, as fast as Fizz ran, he got to Late too late to save Late from his fate. If only Late had been late today, Fizz thought, he would've been on time.

He skidded to a stop to find Percy Late surrounded by Lord Barboozul and a pair of clowns. (They were the last two clowns in the circus who still had their good health and full use of costume, nose and custard: Bongo Bongoton, the mime who taught Fizz English, and Unnecessary Sid, who nobody noticed very much. Normally Sid just stood at the back in the clown routines holding a spare bucket of whitewash, looking at his feet (which took quite a while since, like the feet of most clowns, they were enormous).)

Percy Late was sitting on the floor in the middle of a circle of broken crockery.

Lord Barboozul bent down beside Percy and held out his hand.

'So sorry, old chap,' he said quietly. 'I didn't see you there. I hope you're not hurt. No bones broken?'

'No bones, only bone china,'

said Unnecessary Sid from over his shoulder.

Fizz tugged Bongo Bongoton's sleeve and asked the silent clown what had happened.

Bongo made a spinning motion in the air with one finger, leant back and looked up at where an imaginary plate was twirling majestically above him. Then he held one hand in front of his chin, with the fingers dangling down and fidgeting like seaweed in the swell of the sea, and pretended to walk along. He made the motion of opening a big newspaper and kept walking on the spot while pretending to read it, and then finally he brought his hands together in a banging clap and fell over, folding his arms over his head to protect him from falling imaginary crockery.

'Thanks,' Fizz said, 'that was all I needed to know.'

Percy Late was up on his feet now, dusting down his jacket.

'I'm so sorry about your plate, Mr Late,' whispered Lord Barboozul.

'Oh, it's nothing,' Percy answered, 'I've got dozens of them in there.' He threw his thumb over his shoulder to indicate his caravan. 'I'm always breaking them.'

Fizz watched Lord Barboozul's face very carefully as this information was given, and he was sure he saw a tiny twitch of the cheek. Or he thought he was sure. But then he *wasn't* sure, because the bearded man smiled and slapped Percy Late on the back, saying, 'Well, that's jolly good luck for you, isn't it? Jolly good luck indeed. I'll make a note to remind me to tell my wife. She'll be delighted to know that.

She's a big fan of yours.'

'Really?' said Percy, cheering up. 'Lady Barboozul likes *my* act? You mean *your* Lady Barboozul? With the . . . ? Wow!'

And then the stupid man blushed.

'Keep up the good work, and the plates,' Lord Barboozul said, and he patted Percy on the back again and trotted off, whistling into his beard.

Well, Fizz clearly wasn't going to get any evidence here, so he wandered back to Dr Surprise's caravan to talk over what he had found with the mind reader.

*   *   *

'I don't believe it,' Dr Surprise said when Fizz told him his theory. 'She's such a nice woman.'

'No,' said Fizz. 'She's so not! She stole my mum's nose, and tickled my dad so his back went. And how do you explain the fur ball?'

'Well, it was probably an accident,' Dr Surprise said. 'Flopples probably swallowed it by mistake. She'll nibble anything she can find. See, that's your mystery solved.'

Fizz folded his arms. 'I don't believe that, and neither do you,' he said.

'But, think about it Fizz. Supposing you're right, tell me, *why* is she doing this? Why upset poor Flopples? Why steal Gloria's nose?'

By now Flopples had regained some of her own colour (the vet had given her some large pointy orange pills) and had nibbled the corner of a piece of lettuce fudge. She was going to be alright, but she wasn't up to performing yet. Dr Surprise was still out of the show.

'I don't know, Dr Surprise, but I will find out. That's why I came to see you. I thought you'd help. You're the mind-reader. If we get close to her, can you read her mind and find out? Could you see what she's thinking?'

'Oh Fizz, would that I could, but it doesn't work like that.' He shook his head. 'I'm not a very good mind reader, not when it comes to actually looking *inside*. I'm just a showman. I do tricks. What you need to do is to get her to talk. That's the easiest way of seeing inside someone's mind. You just ask them.'

'But she'll never say,' said Fizz. 'She's not stupid, is she?'

'I don't think so. I mean you've seen their act. That's not the act of a stupid person, Fizz. You'll need the brain of a Sherlock Holmes to catch her out. Not that I think she's done anything wrong.'

'Dr Surprise,' Fizz said after a moment. 'You know you said you couldn't see inside her head? Well, that's given me an idea. If we can't get in her head, I think there's somewhere else I *can* get in.'

Fizz looked around, as if to make sure they weren't overheard and leant in closer to tell Dr Surprise the idea that had just appeared in his brain.

*   *   *

I won't tell you what it is, because that wouldn't be good storytelling. Knowing me, I'll probably explain it all in the next chapter anyway. But right now, I'm going to have a cup of tea and a biscuit. The kind with chocolate on the top (biscuit, not tea, that is). Or if I can't find one of those, then maybe a pink wafer, or possibly a ginger nut, but almost certainly not a cat biscuit, unless I make a terrible mistake in my use of the biscuit barrel. But I've got quite a lot of biscuit barrel experience under my belt and very, very rarely make such mistakes, so don't worry about me. I'll be fine. (Unless the next chapter begins with a 'Meow', in which case, please send for the vet.)

CHAPTER NINE

In which a caravan is searched and in which a conversation is overheard

Fizzlebert Stump was creeping. On tiptoe. With his shoulders down as low as they could go and with his hands held up like little paws. (No one knows why tiptoeing people hold their hands up like little paws, but it always seems to work better that way.)

He was edging round the corner of the Barboozuls' caravan.

Dr Surprise's quavering voice was coming from the other side.

'Um,' it said. 'Lady Barboozul? Your Lordship? I've got a note for you.'

'A note?'

That was Lady Barboozul's voice.

'Er, yes, Your Ladyship,' Dr Surprise said before quickly walking off.

Fizz listened closely as one of the Barboozuls opened the envelope the Doctor had delivered.

127

'What is it?' said Lord Barboozul.

'The Ringmaster,' said his wife. 'He wants to speak to us in his office.'

'What about?'

'The silly man doesn't say. Still, we'd better go see what this is all about.'

Fizz heard the two Barboozuls walk off into the maze of tents and caravans. The Ringmaster's office was right over the other side of the circus. With any luck he'd have at least ten minutes before they came back.

He crept round to the front, went up the steps, looked over his shoulder to make sure no one was watching, and tried the door.

It was unlocked and he slipped inside.

The Barboozuls' caravan was bigger than the one he lived in with his parents. It was neater too.

The front door opened into a little passage. On one side was the kitchen and dining room, on the other side were a pair of bedrooms. Opposite him another door opened into a little toilet and shower room.

He left the bedrooms for later and

128

crept mouse-like into the kitchen.

Plates were neatly stacked on the draining board and there were flowers in a vase on the table. He had been hoping to see a pile of clowns' noses and a pair of large false teeth, with a note attached saying, '*We done it, guv. It's a fair cop!*' but he wasn't so lucky.

The first thing he did was open the kitchen drawers and rummage through them. He had to be as neat as he could, but still be quick about it, while all the time keeping an ear open for the Barboozuls coming back, and an eye open for clues. It wasn't as easy as it sounds.

In the bottom drawer were tea towels. In the top drawer were, as is normal, the knives and forks, but in the middle one was a whole stack of letters and bits of paperwork.

After a quick glance out the window to make sure no one was coming (they had net curtains up, which made it easier to not be noticed inside, but also made it harder to notice what was going on outside, since you had to either squint to see through one of the lacy holes, or lift up the corner and have a look), Fizz heaved the pile of papers onto the kitchen table.

They were bills and letters and boring bits and bobs that didn't interest him.

As far as he could see none of them said, '*This is why we've got it in for the circus, signed Lord & Lady Barboozul*'. It was getting annoying. He'd wasted a good few minutes rooting through that heap.

He put the letters back as neatly as he could and continued looking round the room.

The cupboards were filled with saucepans and tin cans and crockery and all the usual stuff you find in a kitchen, none of which was of any use to him. That was more time wasted. He looked at the clock above the sink. The hands had moved round faster than he expected. He'd have to be even quicker now, searching the rest of the caravan.

The last place to look, in the kitchen, was a big old trunk pushed up against the far wall. When Fizz managed to get the heavy lid up he found it empty except for some old black rag rugs.

Or at least that's what Fizz thought they were at first.

When he looked closer and lifted one of the 'rugs' up it seemed to be made of long black thick hairs, like a wig.

Growing up in the circus he had seen plenty of wigs, but never one quite like this.

For one thing it was long and pretty raggedy, but odder than that was the fact that there didn't seem to be any way to put it on your head. Normally the top of a wig is a bit like an elastic shower cap: it goes on your head like a hat and the hair hangs down. But this wig didn't have anything like that. Instead all the hair was threaded onto a sort of semi-circle of thin material, which had a hole in it. How was that supposed to stay on? he thought.

And then slowly his brain caught up. The semi-circle was a little tacky to the touch. Not sticky *now*, but it gave him the idea that it had been sticky *before*, and then it all fell into place. This wasn't a wig of *head* hair, or not the head hair you normally found on a wig. It was a beard. A fake beard that someone stuck on their chin. The hole was obviously for the mouth.

Of all the things Fizz had thought about them, he'd never suspected that the Barboozuls weren't *actual* bearded people. Never mind all the robbing and breaking and poisoning he reckoned they'd done, which was bad enough, of course, but pretending to have beards . . . Why, that really was the last straw. (No wonder Wystan insisted they eat on their own, if their beards might fall off at any moment.)

With that he decided once and for all that he really didn't like these people. (A trick is one thing, but lying is something quite different.)

As he stood there looking at the beard he heard the door to the caravan open.

He'd been so involved with his thoughts that he hadn't remembered to keep an eye out. His search of the caravan had really only just begun and they were back already.

For a moment Fizz froze.

There is almost absolutely no way you can sensibly explain to someone why you're in their house when they come back unexpectedly. Especially if you're going through their stuff at the time (even if you are doing it for good reasons). So Fizz did the only thing he could think of, which was to hide.

He jumped into the trunk and gently lowered the lid.

'What a stupid little man,' said a voice that was clearly Lady Barboozul's.

Although she wasn't actually shouting, it sounded to Fizz, even through the wooden sides of the trunk,

133

as if she were angry.

Lord Barboozul said something back, but Fizz couldn't make out the words.

'Quite so,' she replied. 'Writing notes one moment and forgetting about them the next. His brain is addled. And to think he's in charge of the whole show. It's amazing it runs at all.'

Again Lord Barboozul mumbled something back.

'Oh, ha, ha,' Lady Barboozul said. 'Well, after today there won't be much of a circus left. The ring will be practically empty tonight. The audience will be *bored*. And we'll be able to write it all off. Job done!'

Wow. This was exactly what Fizz needed to hear. If he could get all this down on tape, then he'd have the evidence he needed to show the Ringmaster that his new star act wasn't all they were cracked up to be.

If only he had a tape recorder.

And wasn't trapped in a trunk with a bunch of dusty beard-wigs.

Lord Barboozul muttered something

and his wife laughed again. It was a cruel laugh, Fizz thought, the sort that suggested she'd just seen a puppy fall off a skateboard and injure itself quite badly, not the sort of laugh you gave when you were hugged by someone with such a fluffy jumper that it tickled your nose.

Then he heard another voice.

'Hello? Anyone here?'

Fizz recognised it immediately, (a) because it was Wystan, and (b) because Fizz wasn't stupid.

'Oh,' said Lady Barboozul, no longer laughing. 'You're back, are you? Gildas was worried.' Gildas was Lord Barboozul's first name, Fizz remembered. 'Where have you been all morning?'

'Just out walking,' the boy said.

'Walking?'

'Yeah, just walking. You know, round the park. That sort of thing.'

'You've been playing football with that horrid little red-haired brat!'

'No, I never.'

'Don't lie to me, Wystan,' she snapped. 'I've seen you. Remember we're here to do a job and then we're gone. There's no point getting soft and sentimental and actually making *friends.*' (She almost spat the word out.) 'You're just an actor. You're my innocent little information gatherer.' She paused, possibly to ruffle his hair annoyingly. Possibly not. 'We'll be gone in the morning. We're booked in at *Frobisher's Freak-O-Rama-Land* all next week. I thought we might go as clowns. How's your juggling? What do you think?'

(Fizz had heard of *Frobisher's Freak-O-Rama-Land*. They were another circus. He'd never actually seen them himself, though. There was only one fact about them that stuck in his mind: *Frobisher's* had the oldest high-wire act in the whole country. Not, to be clear, the act that was established furthest back in the past (it was actually a new act they got just last year), but the chap who did it was one hundred and six years old. It had to be seen to be believed, they said. He walked out on the high wire and, balancing a full sixty feet above the ring, forgot what he was there for and went back again. Fizz hoped that sometime he'd get to see the act himself, but not today, since he was still stuck in a trunk listening to someone else's conversation.)

He was just hoping nobody needed one of these beards.

'We had a fight,' Wystan said, his words tugging Fizz's ears back into concentration.

'A fight?' Lady Barboozul asked. 'With that boy? Make a note, Gildas.'

'Yeah.'

'I hope you won.'

Lord Barboozul said something. Fizz could tell because there was a silence exactly the same length as a sentence.

'No. It wasn't like that. We just argued,' Wystan said. 'He didn't want to play football—'

'Oh, you stupid children,' Lady Barboozul butted in. 'Always arguing about something. It's an age of tantrums. The sooner you grow up the better. I've always said that.'

Wystan was quiet.

It was a different quiet to when Lord Barboozul spoke. It was quieter and

more sullen. And then the bearded boy spoke again.

'He's onto us,' he said.

'What?' Lady Barboozul snapped.

'Yeah,' Wystan went on, 'he says you're trying to break his circus. He says you want to smash it up.'

'What did you tell him? How did he find out? What did he say? Speak up. Spit it out.'

'I didn't tell him nothing. He's worked it out for himself, hasn't he? He's not as stupid as you reckon he looks. I mean, he was bound to cotton on, wasn't he? You've not exactly been subtle here, have you?'

She just laughed, and Fizz shivered.

If only he'd been able to record all this. If only he'd planned better. And then an even worse thought occurred to him.

He couldn't feel his leg.

He had jumped into the trunk as quick as he could and had been sitting awkwardly when he shut the lid, and he was stuck that way, and now one of his legs had gone to sleep. And the only thing that's worse, as you probably know, than a leg that goes to sleep is a leg that starts to wake up again. And Fizz's leg was beginning to do that just about now.

There was a tingling, numb, buzzing feeling all along his muscles and nothing would make it go away. He tried stretching as much as he could and he tried squeezing as much as he could, but it wasn't helping with the pain. And now it was going through that bit when the pins and needles feel like they're on fire and after that it sort of settled down to a dull numb throb, before it finally felt like a real leg again.

Fizz managed to not go, 'Ow!' or to moan or to make any noise at all. He did really well, right up until the point when his leg had finally woken up.

It was then that he shifted to get more comfortable. He only moved an inch or two, but in the pitch darkness his shoe banged quietly against the side of the trunk, just gently, but enough that . . .

'What was that?' said Lady Barboozul.

'What was what?' said Wystan.

There was a pause as the three bearded saboteurs listened.

Then there was a Lord Barboozul-shaped silence.

'Well, I don't care what you think. I definitely heard something,' his wife barked.

'I didn't hear anything,' Wystan muttered.

'Hmm,' Lady Barboozul said. It was the noise someone makes when they don't agree with what you've just said, but can't be bothered to argue the point. 'Very well.'

Fizz heard the noise of chairs scraping on the floor and Lord Barboozul said something. Plates were put on the table. Wystan groaned.

'Tuna sandwiches again?' he said.

They were having lunch. It surprised Fizz that even amongst all the planning and scheming and plotting and arguing that wicked people do, they still had to sit down at the table with sandwiches and lemonade (this was a guess from the fizz of the bottle opening, it might well have been cola or ginger beer, but it didn't matter) and just . . . well . . . have lunch.

And then Fizz sneezed.

It was a dusty trunk, after all, and those old beard-wigs were all hairy. It was bound to happen. And of course, when a boy sneezes loudly in a trunk in the kitchen of his enemies while they're having their lunch, it can only mean one thing.

The end of the chapter.

CHAPTER TEN

In which questions are asked
and in which a boy is dangled

As soon as the sneeze was out Fizz clamped his hands over his nose.

Fizz wasn't a stupid boy and knew he should have done it *before* the sneeze escaped, but this one hadn't given him any warning.

(Some sneezes creep around for a bit first, have a little tickle, have a little sit down, have a little think, while others just jump out feet first without even waving. It is these sneezes, I have had occasion to note, that make the most mess and the loudest noise and require the most apologies.)

As soon as he sneezed a silence fell outside the trunk.

Fizz could imagine the sight. The bearded Lady Barboozul holding a long slim finger up to her fur-framed lips (a flake of tuna caught in the bristling blue-black hair) to tell her two men to keep quiet. And the three of them tiptoeing soft-footed over to where the trunk sat, squat and impossible to ignore against the caravan wall. They'd bend over, wouldn't they, and slowly open the lid. (Did it squeak? Fizz couldn't remember, but knew he'd soon find out.)

It didn't.

The crack of light appeared as he'd feared and was brighter than he expected.

After so long in the pitch dark the light hurt his eyes. For a moment he couldn't see anything but a pair of dark shapes looming above him, and then there were claws round his neck and he was being picked up, lifted into the air.

'You!' hissed Lady Barboozul.

As his vision de-blurred and slowly returned to normal, her beautiful ice cold eyes drilled into him, and her black-blue beard tickled his hands, dangling limply in front of him.

'I suppose,' she said, leaning so close to his face he could smell her beard, 'that you heard our little . . . discussion just then?'

Fizz gulped and nodded and gulped
and shook his head and looked around,
trying to see an escape route, to find an
escape plan.

Lord Barboozul was stood further
down the kitchen in the direction of the
door.

Wystan was behind the bearded
man, half looking at Fizz and half
trying not to. He looked embarrassed
and was twirling his beard between his
fingers.

'Fizzlebert Stump,' the bearded lady
said. 'Spying, are we?'

Fizz had read lots of adventure
stories where the hero got into exactly
this sort of sticky situation, captured

by the villain and interrogated while dangling over the shark pit or vat of acid. And the hero would always be brave and amazingly cool and wouldn't gibber or jabber or gabble or stutter or stammer or wet themselves when faced with the prospect of certain death. Instead they'd say something sharp and witty and funny (and never give any secrets away) and the villain would get angry and careless and drop the hero into the pit or vat, but in such a careless angry way that the hero would somehow be able to escape. And it was all because of the cool collected calm words he used.

So when Lady Barboozul dangled Fizz in her claw of a hand, accusing him of doing exactly what it was he'd been doing, he thought of these books and summoned his strength and spirit up and answered in the only way he knew how.

'Um,' he said.

Lady Barboozul dropped Fizz (aha! the plan had worked, sort of) and turned her head to look at her husband.

'I told you to be careful,' she snapped. 'You and your big mouth, blabbing everything.'

'I'm sorry, my sweet,' said Lord Barboozul. He coughed softly, and a tendril of beard lifted itself and pointed at the clock. 'But dear,' he went on, 'look at the time. The show is about to begin. What are we going to do about this little Stump?'

She held her beard against her chest as she bent down to look at him.

(Fizz was surprised to see he'd been right about the tuna. There was a flake of it caught in the hairs by the side of her mouth.)

'Well,' she said, her eyes glinting cruelly, 'we'll have to keep him here for now. He's not due in the ring this afternoon. Boo hoo. Do you remember, Gildas? His shabby old lion's lost its teeth, and the good Captain never thought of buying a spare pair. No one's going to notice if he's not there. Then, later, after the show, we'll have to make a . . . more permanent decision.'

'So? Back in the trunk?' asked Lord

Barboozul.

'Yes. I suppose that will have to do for now.'

Before Fizz could scuttle out of the way he was gripped round the neck by her sharp fingers, hoisted up into the air and dumped into the trunk.

The lid was slammed down and he heard things being put on top. They sounded like heavy things.

He was back in the dark.

He could hear the Barboozuls moving around in the caravan and even as he banged on the side of the trunk he knew they were no longer paying him any attention.

*　　　*　　　*

After a while it all went quiet.

Fizz thought he heard the caravan door shut but he couldn't be sure. The noise had been quite faint. He waited another few minutes, just to be on the safe side.

Then he banged once more on the side of the trunk.

There was no reply. They must have

gone off to the afternoon show.

So, all he had to do now was escape and go and warn everyone.

He pushed at the trunk lid.

He didn't know exactly what they'd piled on top of it, but it wasn't budging.

He closed his eyes (in the darkness not much changed) and took a deep breath. He was lying on his back, the beard-wigs providing him a pillow, and he thought about what he knew.

He knew which side the hinges were on and he knew that the further away from the hinge you pushed, the more effect it had. So he lifted his feet up and pressed them against the lid, over on the other side, with his knees right up in his chest and he pushed. Still the lid barely moved, but for just a moment there was the slightest chink of light.

That meant it was working.

All Fizz had to do was push harder, and he did so, with both his hands and feet. Remember, Fizz's dad was *The Mighty Stump*, the great circus strongman. For a moment it seemed that just a little of that amazing strength flowed into his son. Fizz

148

pushed a third time and the lid rose slowly, then there came a crashing clatter as stuff fell off and then, with one final shove, the lid was upright.

Fizz clambered out, sneezing once and brushing the dust off his clothes.

There was a mess of things on the floor: crockery, an iron, saucepans and heavy books. Some of the plates were broken, but since he'd seen what Lord Barboozul had done to Percy Late's plate, he didn't feel guilty.

He ran through the kitchen to the caravan's front door, which, this time, they had locked.

He tried putting his shoulder against it and pushing, but even with his junior strongman strength it wouldn't give.

He went back into the kitchen and looked at the windows. They were locked (he couldn't find the key) and were double glazed (he threw a tin can at them, but it just bounced off and rolled under the kitchen table).

He banged on the window anyway, but there was no one passing.

The afternoon show had already begun. Anyone who was still on their

feet would be over at the Big Top by now, trying their hardest to impress the anonymous Circus Inspectors and their clipboards, little knowing that the Barboozuls were working their hardest in the opposite direction.

He sat down at the kitchen table and looked at the remains of the lunch he'd interrupted.

It *was* lemonade (Fizz had correctly guessed the fizz) and he drank some. Then he ate half a tuna sandwich that one of them had left. It was pretty good. In fact, he preferred it to the ones his mum made. (Because Mrs Stump couldn't think of another food which rhymed with tuna (and neither can I), she'd always invite Signore Alberto Volumo, the circus's semi-resident singer of operatic arias, to come and sing while Fizz ate, making them tuna and crooner sandwiches. When it came to fish sandwiches, both Fizz and the neighbours preferred her more straightforward salmon and gammon.)

He thought about the bit of fish he'd seen dangling in Lady Barboozul's beard. And then he thought of the smell of it.

And suddenly a plan popped into his head.

At least he thought it was a plan. It looked a bit like a plan. It was plan-shaped.

It was certainly brilliant, if, by some crazy chance, it actually worked.

All he needed was some tuna.

Fizz looked down at the empty plate.

He looked at his plan again, in his head. His plan just needed some tuna.

He looked again at the empty plate, a sinking feeling in his stomach, and pushed the breadcrumbs round with his finger.

He'd just eaten the tuna.

He felt like a fire-eater who's swallowed an ice cube.

The fate of the entire circus rested in his hands and he'd spoilt his only chance of escape by eating the remains of someone else's lunch. (I expect there's a lesson there (I only mention it on the off chance you're taking notes).) If he couldn't expose the Barboozuls' acts of sabotage to the Circus Inspectors, they'd think that the circus was always like this (dangerous, clumsy, short on acts) and they would almost certainly shut it down. He could just picture the scene as the Inspector pulled the report off his clipboard and gave it to the Ringmaster. He would bark instructions at everyone, even as the Big Top was being dismantled for the last time. All the clowns would have to take their makeup off and go get ordinary jobs, in offices, photocopying and filing. Miss Tremble would have to say goodbye to her horses and become an accountant. Dr Surprise would have to give Flopples away, sell his top hats and become a used car dealer. And Fizz and his mum and dad would be made to live in a house in the suburbs that never moved and he'd have to go to a big grey school where there were no lions, cannons or any sort of fun at all.

The thought of it made Fizz regret eating anything ever.

He slumped in the chair trying to think of a different plan.

But his mind was empty of anything except the dreadful things that would befall the circus if the Barboozuls got away with their rotten scheme. Not a single new plan popped up into his head.

*   *   *

I'm afraid I've got to interrupt this chapter at that point because there's all sorts of other stuff going on around the circus at pretty much the same time that I need to tell you about. It's important stuff and some of it has Fish the sea lion in, and he's always entertaining. I promise we'll get back to Fizz and his despondent leg-swinging just as soon as we've looked around elsewhere.

CHAPTER ELEVEN

In which we go 'meanwhile, over there' a lot

Meanwhile, away across the circus, things were afoot. (Which just means 'happening', not actually 'a foot'. Of course, some things were 'a foot', mainly things on the bottom of people's legs or things which were twelve inches long (such as rulers), but we're not interested in those right now.)

The matinee had begun in the Big Top.

Percy Late had opened the show by spinning his plate.

Bongo Bongoton (the mime) had been stuck inside an invisible box (although he might have been cleaning some invisible windows, or, now I have another look, perhaps he was actually building an invisible cat).

And Unnecessary Sid had fallen off a bicycle. (This wasn't his usual act, but the unicycle had gone missing and he got confused by the second wheel.)

The Ringmaster was stood backstage with his arms crossed and his cheeks pink, hoping that the reduced show would be enough to impress the Circus Inspectors.

He'd cut the stiltless stilt-walkers from the show. They were sad but he had to insist that *just*-walking is not a good enough routine.

In the night, the ropes that held the trapeze forty feet in the air had somehow stretched and although the trapeze artists (the twins, Simon and Simone Vol-au-Vent) were both present and correct and uninjured, the brilliance of their act was diminished by the fact they had their feet on the ground as they performed their breathtaking feats of derring-do. Leaping from one trapeze to the other in mid-flight is less impressive when you can stop to do your shoelace up halfway through, without falling forty feet to the sawdust.

Miss Tremble had woken to find half her horses facing the wrong way. Obviously a backwards horse is no good, she had explained to the Ringmaster slowly and clearly, even as he stood there going, 'But . . . ?!' She'd agreed to allow the four horses who were the right way round to do a shortened routine.

He looked out through the tall curtains and watched as they thundered by, hooves spraying up clods of sawdust, and thanked his lucky stars that he still had the Barboozuls. Their act, he hoped, would be good enough to save them all from the Inspector's chopping block (or clipboard and red pen).

Not only did he have his arms crossed, he had his fingers crossed as well, and if you had looked at his boots, you'd have seen strange lumps down the front of those, where his toes were uncomfortably squashed on top of one another. He needed all the luck he could get, no matter how uncomfortable it made him.

*　　　*　　　*

Meanwhile, in his caravan Dr Surprise

put on his (slightly fizzing) spare top hat.

(Earlier, after he'd given the bearded Barboozuls the carefully crafted letter from the Ringmaster (he'd copied the handwriting exceedingly well, he thought), he'd gone back to his own caravan to hide. He regretted letting the boy talk him into doing it. What if Fizz got in trouble? What if *he* got into trouble? He decided to tuck up in his bed, cuddle poor Flopples and keep quiet. But five minutes later there'd been a knocking on his door which just wouldn't go away.

The Doctor wasn't a coward, but neither was he a brave man. He was that much more common thing, someone in between.

He had stood behind the door and said, 'Who is it? I'm not dressed. You can't come in. The rabbit's just been sick again. You'd best go away. So sorry.'

'It's me, Doctor,' had said the Ringmaster's voice.

'Ringmaster?' asked Dr Surprise.

'Yes. Me. We need you, Doctor, with

or without the rabbit. We need you. The circus is sinking and it's all hands on deck. You have to do something. Please.')

And so now, half an hour later, the Doctor was packing what rabbit-free tricks he could think of into his spare top hat.

He looked down at Flopples, who was still more green than brown, and stroked her head. She just looked up at him with big ears as if to say, 'Don't leave me, Doctor.'

He felt absolutely rotten. But in the Circus the Ringmaster was an absolute ruler (like a King, but with more sawdust), and if he said do something, you probably ought to do it. The Doctor couldn't imagine how he'd impress the Inspectors on his own, but if the Ringmaster believed in him, then he would try.

The Doctor was so busy and so flustered working out what tricks he could do without Flopples that he'd completely forgotten about Fizz and the Barboozuls.

He shut the caravan door behind

him and walked toward the Big Top, where the crowd was already roaring and the band were playing. Ah! He could almost smell their applause. Or worse, he thought slumpingly, their silence.

*   *   *

Meanwhile, away across the circus, somewhere else again, Fish was arguing with a seagull. There was a pile of spilt chips on the grass that the seagull had spotted first, but which the sea lion had decided looked interesting (that is to say, edible) to him too. (Fish had seen the seagull and assumed that a fellow sea creature would be looking for fish too, so he was slightly disappointed to see it was just chips, but still *some* food is always better than *no* food.)

The seagull squawked and flapped furiously at the sea lion.

Fish honked back and showed his teeth.

A sea lion may not have quite as scarily big teeth as a land lion has, but

they are still sharp, pointy, long and filthy. (In fact, they were black, which, although bad news in *your* mouth, is actually quite healthy and normal for a sea lion.)

The seagull grumbled, muttered, squawked and finally flew raggedly off, out of reach of Fish's snapping jaws, leaving the sea lion to enjoy the chips all by himself.

Fish gobbled them up, savouring the rich vinegary flavour, and was left sitting sadly, looking longingly at an empty wrapper.

He was still hungry.

Chips were all very well, but a sea lion like Fish was only really interested in the thing that usually came along with them, the bit that normally appears before the words 'and chips' in the shop sign.

In short, Fish loved fish.

If you could see inside his brain it went like this: *Fish? No. Oh . . . Fish? No. Oh . . . Fish? Yes . . . Mmm . . . More? No. Oh . . .* And so on.

He burped a lazy hazy halibut-burp and lifted his nose in the air.

He sniffed.

He leant his head on one side and sniffed again.

There, what was that?

He sniffed for a third time, with his head cocked on the other side, and then slowly lowered it.

Oh, he'd smelt something. Even above the fishy smell of his own breath, he'd caught the scent of something interesting.

He began waddling between caravans, lifting his head from time to time and snorting a big noseful of air. Oh yes, the scent seemed to say, this is the way! And he'd waddle along just a little bit quicker.

And after a minute or so he stopped

162

waddling, and began flolloping, which is like waddling but faster.

And then he skidded round a corner between two tents and he was almost where his nose had sent him. He flolloped at full speed, right toward the fish smell that was filling his nose, and bang!

There he was with his head stuck through a bit of wood, wolfing down his favourite food.

*   *   *

Back in the Barboozuls' caravan, Fizzlebert had put his plan into action. But hang on, you're probably saying, what plan? When we left Fizz he had reached a dead end. He was locked in with the useful escape-plan tuna sandwich halfway to his stomach. And now he's put his plan into action? This, you're probably thinking to yourself, is not very good storytelling. I mean, it's not been told, has it? So, okay, give me a moment to backtrack a bit and explain what it is that's happened.

As Fizz was sat swinging his legs

163

idly, trying to think of a new plan, his shoe hit something hard. Something hard that rolled away when he kicked it. It was, he saw when he bent down, the tin he'd thrown at the window. It had bounced off and ended up under the table. And what do you think was in that tin? The tin he hadn't read the label of before he threw it? (If you just said 'tuna' you're right and deserve a housepoint (or whatever equivalent writers are able to give to their readers); if on the other hand you said 'sweetcorn' or 'pineapple chunks' then you'd best stay behind after the book for detention as you clearly haven't been paying attention.)

It was tuna! (Da-dah!)

And with the tin of tuna Fizz was able, at last, to put his plan into action, and his plan was this:

(a) He knew he could rely on Fish to track down the source of any fish-flavoured stink.

(b) Fish had a problem being quiet. (He was like a clown with a sensitive horn. He honked and barked all the time. That was simply what he did.)

(c) If Fizz could attract Fish to the Barboozuls' caravan with fish, he could be relied on to make a loud noise outside the door and someone would hear it, know something fishy was going on, and come and force the door open. All it would it take was a couple of riggers with a crowbar and he'd be free.

It was a pretty good plan. Fizz couldn't see a flaw in it. It made sense. It was logical. Give him a few minutes and he'd be out of there.

He used a can opener from the kitchen drawer to get the lid off and poured the tuna-y fish brine on the floor, right at the bottom of the front door. With his fingers he sloshed the juice into the gap underneath the door, and then squidged and squeezed as much of the tuna as he could in there too.

As he squished the fish into the thin slot, it pushed the briny juices even further through and in his mind's eye Fizz could imagine them oozing out the other side and dripping down the caravan's steps, leaking their strong pong into the fresh air.

All he had to do now was wait.

He went back into the kitchen and washed his hands. As he wrapped the tuna can in a plastic bag (they stink out the rubbish and attract flies otherwise (what a thoughtful boy he was)) and went to put it in the bin, he glanced out the window.

What was that?

Oh, it had worked! Already!

There was Fish, flolloping at top speed along the grass between the tents opposite.

Fizz waved his arms and banged on the window, trying to get the sea lion's attention.

'Hey, Fish!' he shouted. 'Go get help! Fish, it's me! Look over here!'

But Fish wasn't paying attention to the boy in the window, and to Fizz's eye it didn't look like he was slowing down either.

And suddenly there was a smashing

166

noise.

Oh, poor Fish, Fizz thought, as he ran back to the door.

But to his surprise all he found was the sea lion's head, poking through a sea lion's head-shaped hole in the bottom of the door slurping and scoffing and wolfing the tuna.

Fizz patted his nose (which is a dangerous thing to do while a sea lion is eating with such abandon—please don't try this at home), and was happy to see that his friend seemed entirely uninjured.

It didn't take Fish a moment to finish the tuna and as soon as he had, he slid backwards out of the hole, ready to start looking for the next meal.

With just a little extra kicking and banging Fizz was able to make the hole big enough to fit through himself and once he was out he shouted, 'Fish, let's get to the Big Top!'

Fish, thinking there might be fish, flolloped along as Fizz ran.

*　　　*　　　*

I should really put some dramatic music here, don't you think? Will they make it to the next chapter in time to save the circus? (*Dum-dede-dum, dum-dede-dum, dum-dede-dum-dum-dum-dum-dum* . . .) Will they even make it to the next chapter in time for the next chapter to start? (*Dum-dede-dum, dum-dede-dum, dum-dede-dum-dum-dum-dum-dum* . . .) Who knows? (I know.)

You know the drill by now. Turn the page for the new chapter, and find out what happens next.

CHAPTER TWELVE

In which a whole load of stuff happens, in and around the Big Top

Fizz was alone when he found the Ringmaster stood behind the backstage curtains. (Fish had been distracted by two halves of hotdogs and another spilt packet of chips on the way. (People are *so* careless with their food sometimes.))

Fizz recognised the music the band were playing as Percy Late's theme.

'I sent him out with a second plate,' the Ringmaster explained, seeing Fizz come running up. 'We're that desperate, lad.'

'Ringmaster,' said Fizz breathlessly. 'I know what's been going wrong. I heard them! They locked me up. They've been stealing everything!'

'Slow down, Fizz. What are you talking about?'

'The beards,' gasped Fizz, still out of breath from running. 'The Barboozuls.

They've been sabotaging the circus. They stole—'

'Now, Fizz,' interrupted the Ringmaster, 'don't tell lies. Lady Barboozul has already told me you might say something like this. I'm afraid she guessed this little fantasy of yours.'

'But—'

'Ever since you lost Charles's teeth you've been upset, and I understand that, but to go pointing the finger and making up stories like this—'

'No, but it's true, Ringmaster! Lady Barboozul stole my mum's nose. And Dad, well, he was tickled, wasn't he? That's what did his back in, what put him out of action . . . and what tickles? Beards tickle! I was hiding in their caravan and I heard them admit it all.'

'Fizz, Fizz, Fizz. I'll get angry in a minute if you keep on with these lies. It's unpleasant to make accusations without proof . . .'

'I've got proof!' Fizz shouted.

'I'd be very interested to see it,' said a smooth, cool voice from right behind his head.

Fizz spun round. There was Lady Barboozul looking down her beard at him.

'You did it all,' he said, before the Ringmaster put his hand on Fizz's shoulder and pulled him back against the buttons of his coat.

'I'm so sorry about the lad,' he said. 'I think he's banged his head on something. His father does leave such heavy things lying around. A caravan can be a dangerous place if you're not careful.'

'Have him taken away, Ringmaster. Now.'

'I haven't got time, Lady Barboozul. I've got a show to run. I'm sure he'll stand nice and quiet over here, out of the way. Won't you, Fizz?'

'No. No, I won't be quiet! She's a liar and a thief and she's trying to ruin our circus!'

'Don't be stupid, Fizz,' the Ringmaster snapped, losing his cool. 'What utter nonsense. The Barboozuls are the only act that's not had to be shortened or cancelled. They're our only chance to impress the Inspectors,

Fizz. Think about that.'

'Yes, we're all that stands between you and the grim world outside, boy,' said the bearded woman.

'So you should be thankful they're here at all, after the things you've said about them. You do want the circus to pass the inspection, don't you, Fizz? And besides,' the Ringmaster went on, softening his tone and smiling at the bearded lady, 'such a nice lady as Lady Barboozul couldn't possibly—'

Just as he began the sentence Percy Late's second plate came rolling out from between the curtains and Percy came running after it.

'Oh blast and bother,' he said as he tried to catch his runaway crockery.

There was the sound of booing from the other side of the curtain. Which is almost as horrible a noise to hear in the circus as a queue of audience members saying, 'Can I have a refund please?' which sometimes comes next.

The Ringmaster rushed through the curtains and they could hear him making jokes and trying to calm the audience down and get them laughing again.

By Fizz's side, Lady Barboozul was hissing at him.

She leant down close over him, grabbed his arm with one of her claw-like hands, and whispered right into his face.

'You little wretch, you vermin, you worm! How did you get free? I do hope you didn't smash a window. You'll pay for it if you did.'

'No, not a window,' Fizz said, standing up to the bully. 'I broke the door.'

She hissed again and poked him with a long finger.

'Oh, you'll be for it soon. Just you wait and see.'

There was nothing she could actually do because there were other people around. Two clowns (Unnecessary Sid and Bongo Bongoton) were playing cards with one of the fire-eaters over on one side, and Percy Late was still chasing his plate in ever smaller circles not far away on the other side.

'Where have you hidden all the things you stole?' he said, loudly.

The clowns were watching with interest. Although they'd heard what Fizz had told the Ringmaster they hadn't decided yet who they reckoned was telling the truth. (Clowns are terrible at making their minds up.)

Underneath their makeup they liked Fizz, of course, they'd known him since he was a little boy. But that meant they also remembered all the times he'd told fibs (there never had been an invasion by Martians) or got in trouble (Madame Plume de Matant had used her powers to divine where the frog in her bed had come from) or had gone missing before (remember *Fizzlebert*

Stump: The boy who ran away from the circus (and joined the library)?). And with their makeup on, well, even if they could make their minds up, there was no guarantee they'd come to a sensible decision.

'I stole nothing,' Lady Barboozul said, standing up straight and putting her hand on where her heart would've been, had there not been a glistening black beard in the way.

She looked at the clowns, shivered slightly, and turned to the fire-eater they were sat with.

'I swear I'm innocent, my good . . . man.'

She said it in such a hurt tone, such a voice of meekness and tender feelings, that Eric Burnes (the fire-eater) nodded with her, and Bongo Bongoton put down his invisible cards and blew his nose on an invisible hanky. (What he meant by this, no one really knew.)

'She's lying,' Fizz shouted. 'Just look at her eyes. They're cold.'

'Now then,' Burnes said, getting up. 'You shouldn't be rude to a lady, Fizz. I think you'd best run along now. Go back to your mum and dad. Go on. Get out of here.'

Fizz didn't move.

Eric picked up a step ladder and started walking towards him.

For a moment Fizz was confused, but then it was clear.

The show was going on. The show always had to go on. This was the circus after all. Everyone mucked in, everyone helped each other out. The fire-eater was preparing the Barboozuls for their opening extravaganza.

From outside the tent Lord Barboozul and Wystan appeared. They'd obviously (Fizz reckoned) been off somewhere causing some last-minute bit of chaos.

Lord Barboozul, at least, looked momentarily shocked to see Fizz.

'Mr Stump,' he said quietly. 'How nice to see you.'

Wystan's face was harder to read because he turned it away.

Even as Fizz protested, the fire-eater helped Lord Barboozul up the ladder and onto his wife's shoulders,

and then Wystan followed. The long coat was done up (with their beards poking through) and as soon as the audience was hushed and their music began they were guided out into the circus ring.

'But, they're . . .' Fizz began, feeling beaten and ignored and lost.

The Ringmaster was back.

'I'm disappointed with you, Fizz. You know how important today is, and yet you try to ruin it all. You know, I'm going to have to talk to your parents about this behaviour. What would they think?'

'But it wasn't me,' Fizz said, limply. 'It was them.' He pointed out at the ring.

'Right,' said the Ringmaster with finality. 'Get back to your caravan. I'm going to have to think long and hard about this.'

He put his hand on Fizz's shoulder and began to lead him out of the tent. Fizz felt defeated, hopeless.

And then, to make him feel even worse, he smelt a smell like old socks. It was the pungent scent of smoked kippers. Fish, who'd finally caught up with him, let out yet another fish-flavoured belch as he flolloped into the backstage area, almost knocking them over.

'Oh, Fish,' the Ringmaster said. 'Your breath doesn't half smell.' He leant down to whisper in Fizz's ear. 'Fizz, you're going on sea lion tooth-brushing duty for the next month. I think that'll teach you some manners.' He stood up again, and Fizz heard him say to himself, 'If we still have a circus, that is.'

He paused as he heard the music change.

Fizz could tell that out in the ring the Barboozuls had disentangled themselves from the triple-decker person that opened their act and were on into the second stage. Wystan would be looking for someone in the audience and Lord Barboozul would still be hidden by smoke.

At that moment, Fizz felt a shove on his thigh.

Fish's head was squeezing between him and the Ringmaster, and he was pushing his way toward the curtain that separated backstage from the ring.

And then suddenly Fish was no longer between them. He was loose.

'Stop that sea lion!' the Ringmaster was shouting, as the sea lion flolloped out through the curtains.

*   *   *

I know that's the end of the chapter, but to be honest, I'm just going to turn over the page and write the next one straight away, so if I were you I'd come with me. Follow that sea lion!

CHAPTER THIRTEEN

In which bad luck befalls
some people and a sea
lion has his moment

As soon as Fish got into the ring he could tell something was wrong.

All he'd done was follow the smell of fish, like he always did, but when he looked around him all he could see was sawdust and these bright lights pointing down at him. They were dazzling.

Then came the laughter.

An audience at a circus who sees an unexpected sea lion in a smart spangly waistcoat flolloping into the middle of the ring, lit up by spotlights and clearly confused, can't help but laugh.

'Catch that sea lion!'

The Ringmaster came running out with Eric Burnes and the two clowns.

'Get him! Before he ruins the . . .'

The four of them stopped as they realised they were suddenly lit up. Unnecessary Sid fell over his long feet, and Bongo Bongoton opened an invisible door and stepped through it. (Put a spotlight on a clown and they do what clowns do.) The Ringmaster ignored them and pulled Eric Burnes' sleeve, saying, 'Come on, let's get that sea lion, before he ruins everything.'

Fizz, now free, seized his chance and ran into the ring too.

Over on the far side the bearded Barboozuls were bravely battling on with their act, while out in the middle of the sawdust the attention-grabbing Fish was busy comically looking over his shoulders.

From one side people were running at him with their arms open as if they wanted to hug him (this happens to a sea lion quite a lot in a circus, especially when spotted by children in the queue. He had his own methods for dealing with unwanted hugs, mostly involving burping) and from the other side came the delicate, faint but unmistakable (to his high-powered nose) aroma of tuna.

It was an easy decision.

He lunged at the bearded trio and,

181

with Eric Burnes hanging onto his tail, fell short.

The audience loved it.

They were laughing and clapping. Nothing had been this funny all afternoon.

A moment later this was the scene: Fish was wiggling in the sawdust, with a bald man with fiery tattoos hugging him tightly round his tail; Fizz and the Ringmaster were stood either side, one shouting, 'Well done Eric, hold him,' and the other shouting, 'Let him go, Mr Burnes, he's trying to save us,'; Lady Barboozul had pulled a fan from her beard and was waving it theatrically at her face, as if to say, 'Crikey, that was a close call,'; and the audience was clapping, thinking this strange interlude in the routine was now over.

A sea lion, however, is a slippery customer and Fish's flight wasn't so easily curtailed.

Fizz could see that the fire-eater was struggling hard to keep hold of the beast, and so he started pushing and shoving him.

'Let him go,' he shouted. 'Get off

him.'

'Get off *me*,' Burnes shouted back.

The man was bigger, heavier and much more burly than Fizz was, and there was no way our hero could push him off if he didn't want to be pushed off.

But then Fizz saw a shape appear at his side.

It was a black shape.

It was a furry shape.

It was an unruly shape.

'What do you think you're doing?' said a voice, low and angry and sharp, but unmistakably Lady Barboozul's.

'Helping,' said a voice from the beard at Fizz's side. The question may have been asked by the bearded lady, but the answer was clearly intended for Fizz's ears.

It was Wystan.

As Fizz watched, the boy's beard wriggled and ruffled around Eric's ear and on his cheek and down the side of his neck. It was tickling him on the flaming tattoo. It looked like a dozen tiny furry fingers flickering through the firelight.

Burnes' hand came up to swat away what he probably thought was just a tickling fly, and it's a truth universally acknowledged that only having one hand on a damp, wriggling sea lion is never enough.

Fish burst out and lunged directly at Lady Barboozul.

She'd left the caravan in such a hurry after imprisoning Fizz in the trunk that she'd forgotten to brush her beard, and that bit of tuna Fizz had seen back then, the tiny fleck of tuna that had given him the idea for his escape for their caravan, that rancid lump of old tuna was still stuck in the coiling blue-black fur.

She screamed and stumbled backwards as the heavy sea lion leant its damp dusty flippers on the shoulders of her beautiful flowing long white dress, and licked at her face.

A sea lion has bad breath. A sea lion has sharp black teeth. And a sea lion has a strong wet rasping tongue, a bit like that of a cat, but twenty times bigger.

Lady Barboozul screamed again and tried slapping at Fish to make him stop.

The audience thought this very funny indeed.

Then two things happened all at once.

Firstly, she stepped backwards and bumped into her husband, who had hidden behind her just in case the sea lion wanted him too, and the pair of them fell over.

(Applause. Laughter.)

And secondly, Fish was left with a mouthful of long blue-black hair. He'd pulled her beard off.

(Laughter. Applause. Someone fell off their seat.)

'What!' said the Ringmaster,

pointing at the denuded lady's chin. 'But!'

He was in shock. The audience was enraptured. Fizz was exhilarated. And Fish was annoyed.

Now, if you or I got a bit of fur stuck between our teeth, it would be awkward, but not impossible, to pull it out with our fingers. But a sea lion can't do this (having no fingers). Instead he can only shake like a wet dog, and shake is exactly what Fish did.

Wystan saw what was going to happen first. He pulled Fizz to the

ground, shouting, 'Duck!'

Over the tops of their heads began flying all the things she'd hidden in her beard.

A bunch of magician's flowers.

An umbrella (which sprang open in the air and drifted down to the sawdust a few metres away).

A ladder. A violin. A teddy bear.

And then other things.

Three small red spheres, which Fizz instantly recognised as being clowns' noses.

Two white plates, which landed on

top of one another and smashed.

A clipboard, which went flying.

A massive pair of false teeth, which bounced off Bongo Bongoton's head, knocking him out. (He was used to being hit by invisible things. A solid object was a new, unlikable and distinctly unfunny experience, he later mimed.)

(But they had bounced! Aha! Fizz knew who those belonged to.)

Another one of Percy Late's plates, which landed on its edge and rolled into the darkness at the back of the ring.

Some long sticks of wood that were probably stilts.

'I told you,' Fizz said to the Ringmaster, as he stood up.

The Ringmaster looked at him with his mouth open, pointing with one hand at the pile of Barboozuls who were still getting up, and with the other at his underpants. (A splinter from one of Percy's plates had flown up and cut his braces, dropping his trousers and getting a huge roar of laughter from the crowd.)

'They . . . I . . . but,' he stuttered.

Percy Late came running out of the darkness, holding his extra plate up, saying, 'Oh, look what I found. It just came rolling past me.' ('Pottery in motion,' added Unnecessary Sid.) And they were followed by others who had seen what was going on in the ring. There were a couple of riggers and the Vol-au-Vents, and Dr Surprise was there with a pair of just-walkers who had caught a brief glimpse of their stilts in flight.

But still the show wasn't over.

Free of the beard between his teeth, Fish had begun balancing things.

No longer was he a sea lion with stage fright. He'd forgotten all about the spotlights and the sawdust. Now he was among friends and just showing off.

He was balancing the lion's false teeth on his nose and was honking loudly in a way that said, 'Look at me, aren't I clever, don't I deserve a treat?'

But Lord and Lady Barboozul had got up off the ground and she was protesting loudly.

'How dare you let this monster get away with such an act of barbarism?' she shouted at the Ringmaster.

'Don't you mean "barber-ism"?' said Unnecessary Sid, loudly.

The Ringmaster was holding his trousers round his middle with one hand, while pointing at her with the other.

'You . . . You . . .' he said. 'It was a false . . . a false . . .' His face was as red as his coat, anger and embarrassment mingling in his high blood pressure. 'I answered an advert . . . it said "bearded family", not "beard-wigged family" . . . I believed you . . .'

Once again Lord Barboozul was stood behind his wife (who, strangely enough, looked rather plain without her beard (and with the dirty torn dress and the sawdust in her hair, which, to be fair, never makes anyone look their best)), and was talking quietly at her.

Fizz could make out some of what he said. 'Actually dear, if you listen to the audience, I think the sea lion's not half bad. He has potential. Maybe we should—'

But she was having none of it.

'This is the worst circus we've ever been involved with,' she snapped.

'You mean,' said Wystan, standing up beside Fizz, 'the worst circus you've tried to ruin.'

'How dare you, you little toad!' she blustered. 'You turncoat! We make our judgements and weed out the weak. We eliminate the useless. We make circuses better! We do it for their own good!'

She spoke with such a loud voice, that everyone was looking at her. Even Fish. (He'd dropped the false teeth.) What Fish was now thinking was: *she* had the last bit of fish, maybe she knows where the next bit is.

And he followed her pointing finger.

And there, at the end of where it pointed, was Wystan, the bearded boy.

Fish lunged, sniffed and lifted Wystan up.

'Argh! What are you doing, you silly sea lion?' he yelped. 'I get sea sick. Stop spinning me!'

Fish was balancing the boy on his nose and twirling him round.

Once again he had the audience in the palm of his flipper. They 'oohed' and then they 'aahed' and then they laughed and clapped as Wystan was spun round ever faster.

'Fish,' the Ringmaster said. 'Put . . . put . . . put the boy down.'

Fish ignored him.

Lord Barboozul had pulled a clipboard from his beard and was making notes as he watched. Lady Barboozul was scowling and rubbing her bald, but slightly sticky, chin, and poking her husband with her free hand. It seemed she didn't approve of his writing.

'Oi mate,' one of the riggers tried. 'Drop the kid, would'ya?'

Fish ignored him too. He was having too much fun being the centre of attention.

'Fish,' said Fizz, fumbling in his coat pocket, 'I've got something here . . .'

And he pulled out the empty tin of tuna. The one he'd used to attract Fish in the first place. He'd wrapped it up in a plastic bag and had meant to drop it in the bin, but when the sea lion had

192

broken down the door, everything had got a bit tense and urgent and he'd forgot all about it.

Now he took it out of the bag and waved it in Fish's face.

With a flick of his head, the sea lion tossed the bearded boy over his shoulder and made a snapping lunge for the tin can.

That wasn't exactly what Fizz had hoped for. He didn't want anyone to get hurt. And Wystan *had* helped him get Fish free.

He watched as Wystan flew through

the air.

So did everyone else.

The entire audience watched him, following the arc of his flight with their heads.

Even the de-bearded Lady Barboozul had her eyes in the air.

So engrossed was she in the parabola Wystan's flight followed that she forgot to move out of the way until he'd already landed on her.

She was knocked backwards, slipped on a clown's red nose, and fell straight into Lord Barboozul.

(Laughter. Applause.)

Or rather, I should say, not actually into Lord Barboozul at all. Instead, the correct words are: 'into Lord Barboozul's beard'.

She slipped and tumbled inside, vanishing, her feet wiggling in last of all and sliding down out of sight as if she were falling a great way in there.

A last shout was heard: 'I'll get you, you rotten flea-bitten worm of a . . .' and then there was silence.

Almost silence. Fish burped a waft of haddock-breath as he licked the very last bit of tuna out of the corner of Fizz's tin and with a flick of his tongue threw it in the air, bounced it on his nose, flipped it to his tail and whacked it out of the way.

Fizz and the entire audience watched the spinning tin glinting in the spotlight and then falling down, down, down toward the ring, where it hit Eric Burnes, the fire-eater, right on the very top of his head.

Now we all know that fire-eaters are dangerous people to just leave lying around and when he went 'Ow,' (which is what anyone would say when hit by a flying tin, no matter how tough they were) he let out a small puff of red flame, the very end of which happened to catch the tip of Lord Barboozul's beard.

Before anyone knew what was happening there was a ripping sound as he tore the beard off his face (it was stuck on with theatrical gum, which is strong stuff) and a whooshing sound as the whole beard vanished in a frazzling gust of fire. Wooof! And it was gone. (Hair burns very fast. Do not try to test this at home. Just trust me on it.)

'Ah,' he said quietly, looking at the pile of ashes where the beard containing his wife had been.

The audience went wild with their applause, assuming it to be a brilliant trick of some sort.

The Ringmaster had enough sense to signal to the band to play the closing music and to the stunned crew that they should lift the tent-flaps and let the crowd out.

*   *   *

Well, it only remains for me to tie up the loose ends and explain everything that's happened. Easy enough. I'll do it in the last chapter. (I probably should've done it in the first chapter, which would've made this a much shorter book, but I forgot. Sorry.)

CHAPTER FOURTEEN

In which we reach the end

Once the audience had been emptied out of the Big Top a circus meeting was called.

Fizz's mum got her nose back.

Captain Fox-Dingle brought Charles in and they refitted his rubber teeth.

The stilt-walkers climbed back up and high-fived one another. (They'd spent a whole day low-fiving and hadn't liked it one bit.)

*　　　*　　　*

While Fizz explained to everyone what he'd overheard (to a chorus of gasps and 'Well I never's), Lord Barboozul stood quietly by.

'Why did you do it?' asked the Ringmaster.

Lord Barboozul folded his arms and kept his mouth shut, but Wystan wasn't so unwilling to explain.

'Ringmaster, they're your dreaded Circus Inspectors. That's why they did it all.'

The Circus Inspectors? *They* were the Circus Inspectors? This news got a bigger gasp from the assembled circus crowd than even Fizz's story had.

'But why the sabotage then?' Fizz asked. 'Why all the stealing and breaking?'

'That's their way,' Wystan explained. 'I've listened to Lady Barboozul often enough. She always said, "It's no good coming on a sunny day when everyone's happy. You must see a circus put on a show in the most unpromising of conditions. It's a trial by fire."' At the word 'fire' everyone looked at Eric Burnes who kept his mouth shut, just puffing a little smoke out of one nostril. 'They smash the circus up to see if it still works, to see if you can make it work. If you can survive. I've seen it before, dozens of times.'

'But why didn't you say anything?' asked Fizz. 'Why didn't you let me know?'

'How could I? What I told you about my mum and dad, about them dying in a hot air balloon, that was true, Fizz. You've got to believe me. The Barboozuls really did take me in. So I had to do what they said. Otherwise, where would I go? What choice did I have? I'm sorry. I'm really sorry I did it, but . . .'

The Ringmaster turned to Lord Barboozul and said, 'Is this true? Are you really the—'

Lord Barboozul tapped at his clipboard and interrupted. 'Ringmaster, you know how it is. A Circus Inspector is an anonymous figure. No one knows who they are. So, if I were one I couldn't tell you, could I? I certainly wouldn't admit it. And by telling you anything at all this little wretch has broken every code in the Circus Inspector's rulebook. I expect. I wouldn't know, though, because obviously I'm not a Circus Inspector. Am I?'

'Yes you are,' Wystan said. 'He is.'

'I believe you,' said Fizz. 'Just look at him, of course he's the Inspector. He's got a clipboard.'

Lord Barboozul turned on Wystan unpleasantly and said, 'Well, what are you going to do now, you little freak? You'll never get to be an Inspector. Once I let them know what you've done, you'll be shunned for the secrets you've spilt. I expect. I mean, if I knew who to tell. Which I don't, because I'm not one. Anyway, I certainly don't want you hanging round on my coat-tails any more. I always said you were more trouble than you were worth. The money we had to spend on shampoo. She's the one who knew your mother and—'

'I don't know what I'll do,' Wystan said loudly. 'I guess I'll . . .'

'He's staying with us,' Mrs Stump said.

'What?' said Fizz.

'What?' said Wystan.

'I mean what I say. He can stay here with us in the circus.'

Fizz looked at his mum. She didn't have her clown face on, so he knew she was being serious.

'Bah,' said Lord Barboozul. 'Who'd

200

want a little freak like that hanging round?'

'He's not a freak,' said Fizz. 'He's just a kid.'

'With a *beard*, Stump,' mocked the ex-bearded Lord.

'Don't be silly, I saw the fake beards. We all did,' answered Fizz. 'You locked me in a trunk with them, remember?'

'Actually,' said Wystan quietly, 'this one's real.'

Fizz turned and said, 'It's just stuck on with gum, I saw them,' and gave Wystan's beard a tug.

'Ow! Fizz, stop it.'

'Yes, Fizz, leave the poor chap alone,' said his mum.

'It's real?' said Fizz.

'Yeah. I think that's why Lady Barboozul took me in. I've always been hairy, and it gave her the idea of the act. She said it reminded her of the real circuses in the old days. But *he* never liked it.' Wystan gestured over at Lord Barboozul who'd been standing behind him, but when everyone looked they saw an empty space, more or less the same size as the Lord-cum-Inspector,

but which didn't have him in it.

He'd vanished.

'Looks like you'll have to stay with us then,' the Ringmaster said, and Fizz put his arm round Wystan's shoulder saying, 'Yeah, I think so too.'

Wystan smiled, and then laughed, and his beard ruffled happily in the air.

No one left knew how the magic beards worked, or where their magic pockets went. (Wystan's own beard was just a normal beard, a little wriggly sometimes, but made of normal hair.) Where Lady Barboozul had gone when she fell in, no one, not even Dr Surprise, could work out.

*   *   *

The following morning Flopples was much better. She and the Doctor performed together on Sunday evening. She was brilliant.

Mr Stump was up and around by the middle of the following week, though only tearing telephone directories in quarters.

Mrs Stump's new nose arrived on the Friday and from then on she had two red noses and was called by some of the other clowns 'Two Nose Stump', which was a bit annoying, but then clowns are quite annoying already, so it wasn't a problem.

*   *   *

Wystan had rather enjoyed being picked up, balanced and flipped about by Fish, he said, and if he could wear his crash helmet then it would probably be safe enough to do every night. And

Fish, it seemed, had discovered a newfound sense of show business. He didn't object to balancing things in the ring, so long as there were fish involved at some point. And so, a whole new act was born.

Fizz carried on being the boy with a lion, which carried on wowing the crowds.

At first he'd been jealous of Wystan, but once, when Fizz had a cold and was unable to go on, the new boy star put his head in Charles's mouth. The old lion got upset by the sight of the beard, and then it tickled his nose and then he sneezed, and when he sneezed his teeth fell out. It had been quite funny, but a lion act isn't meant to be funny.

Both Captain Fox-Dingle and Charles were much happier when Fizz was back the next evening.

'Boy. No beard. Better job,' the Captain declared.

On the other hand, when Charles felt under the weather, Fizz would put on one of the Barboozuls' spare fake beards and then there would be two bearded boys in the circus, juggling, tumbling, balancing and doing daring deeds of derring-do with the sea lion. That was a good show.

*   *   *

And one Monday morning the Ringmaster received a large brown envelope in the post. It was stamped with the seal of the British Board of Circuses. He opened it with trembling fingers and pulled out the piece of paper from inside.

It read: '*Circus report mark: C+.*'

Well, it was a pass. It wasn't brilliant, but they'd passed.

Whatever else you could say about Lord Barboozul (unpleasant, cheating, child-hating liar, for example) at least he did his job professionally, the Ringmaster said, and didn't let his personal feelings get in the way.

There was an additional note at the bottom: '*Sea lion act:* Promising.'